"I Kne[~~~]
Blurted[~~~]
[~~~]Into Her Briefcase.

"What?"

"Men don't take the university sex study very seriously," she went on, unable to control herself. "One anonymous male wrote on his volunteer form that he made love one hundred times per day, *eight* days per week. By any chance, was that you?"

Zane's grin came slow and easy. "Sex can make a man say wild things," he said. "Like when I have sex with a woman, she can make me forget where I am, what day it is or even who I am. Does sex with a man do that to you, Professor?"

"Me?" she asked, taken aback. "I—I—" How could she tell him that sensual pleasure was like a fever to her—hot and dangerous. And that it was sex that destroyed her engagement.

Dear Reader,

This month, we begin HOLIDAY HONEYMOONS, a wonderful new cross-line continuity series written by two of your favorites—Merline Lovelace and Carole Buck. The series begins in October with Merline's *Halloween Honeymoon*. Then, once a month right through February, look for holiday love stories by Merline and Carole—in Desire for November, Intimate Moments for December, back to Desire in January and concluding in Intimate Moments for Valentine's Day. Sound confusing? It's not—we'll keep you posted as the series continues…and I personally guarantee that these books are keepers!

And there are other goodies in store for you. Don't miss the fun as Cathie Linz's delightful series THREE WEDDINGS AND A GIFT continues with *Seducing Hunter*. And Lass Small's MAN OF THE MONTH, *The Texas Blue Norther*, is simply scrumptious.

Those of you who want an *ultrasensuous* love story need look no further than *The Sex Test* by Patty Salier. She's part of our WOMEN TO WATCH program highlighting brand-new writers. Warning: this book is HOT!

Readers who can't get enough of cowboys shouldn't miss Anne Marie Winston's *Rancher's Baby*. And if you're partial to a classic amnesia story (as I certainly am!), be sure to read Barbara McCauley's delectable *Midnight Bride*.

And, as always, I'm here to listen to you—so don't be afraid to write and tell me your thoughts about Desire!

Until next month,

Lucia Macro

Senior Editor

Please address questions and book requests to:
Silhouette Reader Service
U.S.: 3010 Walden Ave., P.O. Box 1325, Buffalo, NY 14269
Canadian: P.O. Box 609, Fort Erie, Ont. L2A 5X3

PATTY SALIER
THE SEX TEST

SILHOUETTE *Desire*

Published by Silhouette Books

America's Publisher of Contemporary Romance

For my wonderful husband, lover and best friend, Edward, and for my extraordinarily gifted children, Diana and Jeff.

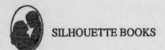 SILHOUETTE BOOKS

ISBN 0-373-76032-9

THE SEX TEST

Copyright © 1996 by Patricia Bury Salier

This edition published by arrangement with Harlequin Books S.A.

Printed in U.S.A.

PATTY SALIER

Born and raised in Gravesend, Brooklyn, in New York, Patty credits her mother for her keen logic and her father for her curious, creative mind. She has been a published writer for many years. To Patty, her wonderful husband and two great children are everything she could ever want in life. "I've got so much to be thankful for."

Patty will enjoy hearing from her readers. Send a self-addressed, stamped envelope to P.O. Box 66816, Los Angeles, CA 90066.

A Letter from the Author

Dear Reader,

I was thrilled when Lucia Macro telephoned me from Silhouette Books in New York to say, "Patty, we want to buy *The Sex Test*." I calmly and professionally replied, "That's wonderful," got off the phone and then cheered, hooted and happily burst into tears. "I sold it! I sold it!"

Actually, I've been a published magazine writer for years. I've sold my short stories to confession-story magazines such as *Intimate Story, Personal Romances, True Life Secrets* and *True Confessions*. But I've always dreamed of writing a romance novel, especially since I'm a major romantic.

With two great kids, I'm still wildly in love with my husband, *and* I love to sensually fantasize.

While writing *The Sex Test*, I had fun imagining myself as a professor doing a sex study on the nineties single male. I immensely enjoyed falling in love with my hero as I probed his male psyche for his innermost erotic secrets.

To me, the best part of writing *The Sex Test* was creating a heroine who realized that her fantasies and passionate desire for the man she loved were totally and completely natural.

I hope you enjoy reading *The Sex Test*, because I loved writing it!

All my best to you,

Patty Salier

One

The telephone number Professor Rachel Smith had dialed rang and rang in her ear.

The textbook-filled office she shared at the university with her friend, Professor Kim Woods, suddenly seemed so stuffy and cramped that she could barely breathe.

"He's not answering, Kim," Rachel said tensely as she gripped the white telephone. "Maybe I should hang up."

"You haven't given the man a chance to get to the phone," her friend said. "Will you relax?"

"I can't," she said, the dreaded ringing hauntingly echoing through her head.

She couldn't even sit still. She abruptly stood up at her desk, fighting the urge to disconnect the phone before he answered.

"Kim, I can't do this!" Rachel screeched as she heard the ringing stop and his phone being picked up.

"Zane Farrell's residence," an out-of-breath male voice resonated in Rachel's ear. "How can I help you?"

The deep sensual tone of him momentarily made her heart leap.

"Ahhh, hello, can I speak to Zane Farrell?" she stammered, helplessly glancing at Kim for support.

"Are you bringing me good or bad news?"

Rachel looked at Kim questioningly. Kim immediately leaned her head against Rachel's to listen in.

"Mr. Farrell, I'm Professor Rachel Smith at State University. I'm calling regarding the university sexuality research study."

"A *sex* study?" His manly voice deepened with sudden interest. "You're kidding, right?"

Rachel exchanged a confused glance with Kim.

"Mr. Farrell, I'd like to set up an appointment to come over to your house. Our first interview should take no more than an hour."

"Wait a minute, wait a minute," he said, sounding astounded. "You want to come over *here* and ask me questions about my sex life?"

"Don't you recall, Mr. Farrell?" she continued. "You volunteered for the study by E-mailing your résumé to the university. We're doing research on the sex lives of the nineties single male. I'd like to discuss with you—"

"Oh, I get it," he interrupted. His voice lightened, as if he was smiling over the phone. "You're trying to scam me, right?"

"What?" she bellowed, insulted that he was doubting her sincerity. "I certainly am *not!*"

"Come on, *Professor,*" Zane stressed with a chuckle. "Admit it. You're a radio talk-show host. Am I close? And you're trying to entice me into making sexual innuendos over the air to titillate your listeners."

She angrily grabbed his résumé from Kim. "Is this Zane Farrell at 312 Crescent Road in Bel Air?"

"Right name, right address," he replied. He lowered his voice like he was telling a secret. "But I refuse to tell you the shade or size of my cotton briefs."

"How dare you!" Rachel blurted. Her heart was hammering. Her blood pressure was soaring. "I'm not scamming you, Mr. Farrell. If you'd stop being a pigheaded—"

"Rachel!" Kim called out, pulling the phone away from her. "You're representing the university."

"But he's ridiculing me!"

"Just talk him into the interview," Kim insisted.

Rachel angrily grabbed back the phone. "Mr. Farrell," she began, trying to suppress her fury. "I have your résumé right in front of me. You graduated from high school at fourteen years old. You received your master's degree and Ph.D. by age twenty-four. Now you're an entrepreneur who owns PLT Corporation, Zantic Corporation, and Afloment Industries."

"Did I really do all that?"

He was impossible! "Mr. Farrell, I'm not sure why you E-mailed your business background instead of the personally-slanted bio we requested, but that's your business. However, if you are *afraid* to participate in our sex study—"

"Who's afraid?"

"Are you still interested, Mr. Farrell?" She inwardly gloated that she'd finally gotten to him the same way he'd gotten to her.

"I'm one hundred percent intrigued." Then, in a bass voice almost in an intimate whisper, he added, "Will you ever forgive me for doubting you, Professor Smith?"

The warmth in his voice. His lips seemed so close to the phone that Rachel could almost feel his breath on her face. A pleasurable tingle radiated through her veins. She quickly looked away from Kim, embarrassed by her sensual reaction to him.

"There's no need to apologize…" she began, clearing her throat.

"How could I have let my memory lapse on such an important project?" he went on. "I'll be glad to assist you in every way I can."

Kim shot her a satisfied smile, but Rachel didn't return it. She got the distinct feeling that Zane Farrell was still goofing on her.

"When can we set up a time to meet?" she asked, preparing herself for his next smart-alecky remark.

"How about right now?" he suggested with an enthusiasm that both irked and excited her.

"Now?" she repeated.

"Sure. I'm very eager to find out what your sex test is all about."

She glanced uneasily at Kim who mouthed, "Take him up on it."

"Well, I—" she stammered, plopping down in her chair.

"Great! I'll be waiting for you." Then he hung up.

"Kim, I'm not going!" Rachel said, slamming down the phone and turning Zane Farrell's résumé facedown on her desk.

"You've got to," her friend insisted. "You were given three case studies, and Zane Farrell is one of them."

"He's already making it difficult for me," she said, exasperated. "This is my first research project for the university. I want to do good, Kim. Why, oh, why did the topic have to be *sex?*"

"I can't believe you're complaining." Kim stared at her incredulously. "I know five female professors who begged on their knees for this assignment, but you were lucky enough to be chosen by the administration."

"Lucky?"

"You can't fool me, Rachel Smith," Kim said. "I know *exactly* the reason you're doing this sexuality study on the nineties single male."

"Why?"

"Because you want to meet the sexiest, hottest men in Los Angeles, that's why."

"Oh, no, definitely not!" She blindly fiddled with the case-study folders on her desk, suddenly aching inside.

Kim studied her. "Rachel, you've got to forget what happened with you and Kent. That was two whole years ago."

"I'm over Kent," she insisted. "I really am." And she was. Kent was out of her system for good.

"Then why aren't you dying to meet a great guy?"

Rachel opened her mouth to speak, but the words wouldn't come out.

Even though Kim was her best buddy, she'd never told Kim the real reason that Kent had called off their wedding only three days before the ceremony. She was too ashamed and humiliated by what she'd learned about herself.

"I'd better not keep Mr. Farrell waiting." Rachel quickly grabbed her briefcase. "I don't want him catching a cold in his cotton briefs."

After the phone call with Professor Smith, he barreled up the lavender-carpeted steps of the Bel Air mansion three at a time into the master suite.

He yanked off his oil-stained coveralls and work shirt and hurled them through the open master-bathroom door onto the tile floor.

"Man, oh, man, what the hell did I get myself into?" he said out loud in frustration. The professor's telephone call had totally blown him away.

He grabbed a neatly pressed white shirt and clean jeans and rushed into the bathroom.

As he turned on the shower spray, he replayed her conversation. He couldn't believe it. A sex study? Jeez! He'd never talked about his sex life with anyone in his entire life.

Sure, he'd kidded around with Professor Smith over the phone about talking sex, but the reality of the idea bashed into his sense of privacy. It was outrageous of her to expect him to answer even one question about how his loins functioned.

Why didn't he immediately turn down the sex interview with her? He knew why. It was that velvety voice of hers that got to him. She'd sounded slightly unsure and a bit nervous talking to him. And she'd had a fiery reaction to his sense of humor that had instantly appealed to him.

He adjusted the steamy hot water the way he liked and stepped naked under the sizzling spray. He thought his taut muscles would relax under the wet heat. But he was tenser than ever.

Why had he said yes to that sex interview? Had his brain completely collapsed? He couldn't take part in that study.

How could he let Professor Rachel Smith ask him sex questions? She was expecting to hear the sexual ins and outs of Zane Farrell.

But he had one very monumental problem. He was *not* Zane Farrell!

Rachel chugged her mint-green Valiant up the winding road of wealthy Bel Air. The Los Angeles September air pushed into her open car window like a gush of oven-burning heat.

She lifted the spaghetti straps of her dress off her burning shoulders. She was hot not only from the dry Santa Ana wind coming from the desert.

She couldn't stop thinking about the rich timbre of Zane Farrell's voice over the phone, and the sexy tease of his words. Her sensual reaction to just a phone call with him made her feel even more uneasy about his interview. How could she feel comfortable asking him personal sex questions if she was turned on by him?

As she drove past vast estates of lush green pine trees and walled-in properties, she kept one careful eye on the curvy Bel Air road and glanced at Zane Farrell's address on her dashboard.

Rachel stopped her Valiant in front of a wrought-iron gate that seemed to tower as high as the wall separating King Kong from the jungle villagers. Out of her driver's window, she pressed the black buzzer pad, signaling her arrival.

She spotted the eye of a video camera zooming in on her. She impulsively touched her brown bun at the back of her head. She quickly smoothed her damp dress across both thighs to appear university-like. Moving her hands to the steering wheel, she wished she could stop them from trembling as she held on to it.

The iron gate grinded open to welcome her onto Zane Farrell's estate. She wasn't afraid of entering the unknown property of this stranger. Before their interviews, all sex-study volunteers were followed up with thorough behind-the-scenes investigations into their character. Zane Farrell had checked out as an honest, law-abiding, very, *very* rich citizen.

With brown leather briefcase in hand and suddenly dizzy with excitement about her first interview, Rachel eagerly pressed the square-lit doorbell of the double copper front doors.

Just then, the doors flew open like a hurricane wind.

"Well, hello," said that familiar deep male voice.

"Zane Farrell?" she asked, wonder-struck. She had to blink five times at the six-foot solid frame of the thirty-something man in front of her.

"You've got the right door," Zane Farrell replied with a smile that sent laugh lines sprouting from the sides of both twinkling eyes. "Have I got the right professor?"

"Wh-why, yes," she quickly said.

A pair of Pacific Ocean blues gazed down into hers so intensely that her insides melted like butter in the sun. His smile was warm and confident. He had curly black hair that yearned to be twirled around her fingers. And a muscular body under that white shirt and jeans that put her breath on major hold.

When Zane's twinkling sea-blues glided from her breasts down to her bare legs, she felt her nipples harden against the cotton fabric of her dress at his visual caress. She momentarily fantasized his masculine fingers slipping down her spaghetti straps and crushing her bare breasts with his hands.

Her face flamed at her sensual thoughts. What was with her? She'd barely met the man.

"So you're here to put my libido under the investigative light, are you?" Zane pondered out loud. He extended a massive hand to her. "I hope I don't disappoint you."

"I'm sure you won't," she replied, trying to appear totally in control.

But when she slipped her small hand into his large palm, his grip was firm, warm, and she felt a hot electric current slam straight through her body.

She quickly disengaged her hand from his. Why was Zane Farrell having such a powerful effect on her? No man had grabbed her insides that tight—not even Kent.

Zane leaned his strong hands on each side of the door frame only inches from her, only inches from caressing her. She felt compelled to leave that instant.

"I didn't mean to rush you into this interview," she told him in an unsteady voice. "We could hold it at a more convenient hour for you."

"Absolutely not," he said with welcoming warmth. "I'm looking forward to this." He released one hand from the door frame and stepped aside for her entry. "Please, come in."

As Rachel slipped by him, her shoulder brushed against his hard-muscled chest. He smelled of soap and musky after-shave. She wouldn't stay for long. She definitely *couldn't* stay for long.

"Make yourself at home," he suggested. "The staff's on vacation, so feel free to roam. I'll get us something cool to drink."

Once alone in the kitchen, he frantically searched Mr. Farrell's refrigerator for a beverage to serve her. The compartment was empty except for a half carton of low-fat milk. Jeez! He was nervous enough trying to make the right Mr. Farrell impression, but milk?

He grabbed for the milk container. How the hell was he going to pull off this sex interview? He had no other choice, did he? He was obligated by a commitment he'd made to the real Zane Farrell—a commitment he couldn't break.

As he frantically sifted through the unfamiliar kitchen cabinets for glasses, he flashed on Rachel Smith's inviting brown eyes that had sucked him right in. And her voice rang of honey-sweetness that he found irresistible.

Man, oh, man, he'd better keep himself in check. It wasn't going to be easy pretending to be someone else with a beautiful woman like the professor about to ask him probing intimate questions. He didn't feel one iota comfortable about this sex-test business, especially since he had to act as if it was Mr. Farrell's sexual preferences she was studying, when it would actually be his own!

Rachel set her briefcase down on the oval glass coffee table. She tried to breathe normally again. Zane Farrell was not supposed to be charming, friendly *and* a hunk! How was she going to ask him personal questions about his sex life when she was fantasizing about being an integral part of it?

She had to get a grip. She was at his mansion purely for academic research. She couldn't allow her sudden overwhelming attraction to possess her and ruin her first research project for the university.

Rachel walked to the sliding glass door overlooking a sparkling green kidney-shaped swimming pool. Her attention landed on the inviting Jacuzzi beside it.

She had a fleeting image of Zane's strong nude body pressed snugly against her nakedness as they soaked in the warm, foaming, swishing—

"So, Professor Smith, what do you want to know about my sex life?" Zane's bass voice sizzled through her like a lit Fourth of July sparkler.

She whirled to find him staring at her with intensely interested eyes. His hands were holding two glasses of milk.

"Milk?" she asked, looking at him sideways, suppressing a grin.

"I need to revitalize my body for your sex test," he said, almost as if he was slightly embarrassed.

That little-boy quality captured her. But she couldn't help being very, very aware of him as a full-grown man. Without thinking, her eyes wandered down his very vitalized muscular frame. Her gaze stopped dead center on his tight jeans that accentuated his generously manly bulge. She quickly diverted her focus to the masterpiece paintings on the wall.

Why, oh, why, hadn't she fought harder against participating in this sex research project? It wasn't for her, oh no, not for her.

"We don't have to jump right into the interview," she quickly told him.

"From your phone call, I got the idea you want some major erotic details," he began. "Like the way I—"

"Before we get into any specifics," she conveniently cut in, "I'd like to get a solid sense of your male identity." Her fingers were trembling as she searched through her briefcase for his résumé. "I believe you received your master's degree from—"

"Harvard," he filled in.

She finally found his résumé and frowned. "But your curriculum vitae lists Yale University."

"Right, right," he said. "I always get those two places mixed up."

"Really?" she asked. "I thought a semi-genius like you would hold your university affiliations in high regard."

"Nah," he said. "I tend to file away my past and concentrate on current pertinent data. Like, for instance, your being here with me to examine my sexual need for the female species."

"Ahh—why don't you show me your house?" she suggested, avoiding his twinkling direct gaze. *That's it,* she told herself. *Keep the conversation safe, neutral, and on more wholesome topics.*

But how long could she delay her sexy questions?

Zane studied her for a long moment. "Maybe I'm dead wrong," he began, "but am I making you nervous, Professor Smith? Because if I am—"

"No, no, I'm fine," she insisted. "I have no problem with—"

"Asking what turns me on in bed?" he boldly finished. His eyes were playing with her, teasing her, daring her.

Why, he was definitely getting pleasure from her uncomfortableness!

"I knew this would happen," she blurted out, shoving his résumé back into her briefcase.

"What?"

"Men don't take the university sex study very seriously," she went on, unable to control herself the way Kim had advised. "One anonymous male wrote on his volunteer form that he made love one hundred times a day, *eight* days a week. By any chance, was that you?"

She was *not* going to let this man with the soaring IQ challenge her ability to competently complete her first interview.

Zane's grin came slow and easy. "Sex can make a man say wild things," he said. "Like when I have sex with a woman, she can make me forget where I am, what day it is, or even who I am. Does sex with a man do that to you, Professor?"

"Me?" she asked, taken aback. "I— I—" How could she tell him that sensual pleasure was like a fever to her—hot and dangerous. And that it was sex that had destroyed her future marriage to Kent.

"Hey, it's okay," Zane quickly added. "You don't have to answer." There was a sudden caring in his voice that she couldn't help noticing. "How about I give you a tour of the house?"

"Sure," she said, relieved. Though she couldn't completely figure him out, for that second, Zane had somehow tuned into a painfully vulnerable place in her that no one had ever been aware of but her.

She felt a sudden closeness to him that she hadn't felt with a man in a very long time.

Zane led her through a long Mexican-tiled hallway. She heard his footsteps echo beside hers as though they strolled through a huge cathedral.

"Do you live here all alone?" she heard herself ask. That question was not a requirement on her study list. "I mean— this place is so huge."

"It's just me," he replied. "What about you? Do you live by yourself, Rachel?"

Hearing his deep-toned masculine voice utter her first name sent a warmth of intimacy through her. Suddenly he stopped walking and leaned against the hallway wall, watching her with greater interest than that of an ordinary interviewee. Was he thinking of asking her out? She caught herself secretly hoping he was.

She immediately straightened her spine and tightened her grip on her briefcase. What was she thinking? She was a professor on an interview. She couldn't let herself get personal with him.

"Actually, my non-professional life is irrelevant to the study," she told him.

His eyes held hers. "Maybe to the study, but not to me."

She nervously bit her bottom lip. At that moment, she yearned to share with him whatever he wanted to know about her, things she'd never told anyone else. Somehow, she felt that maybe he'd understand. But she knew her job didn't permit it.

She cleared her throat. "I don't see how my living condition affects this research study."

"It's very simple," he explained. "You want me to get relaxed enough to reveal myself to you, right?"

"Yes," she hesitantly replied, wondering what he was leading up to.

"How can I?" He leaned a little closer to her. "I need to get to know you better, don't I?"

She swallowed. "I see your point." She was trying very hard to act cool and professional, but deep inside, oh, how she wanted him to get to know her better. "I live alone just like you."

"Ah-ha," he mused aloud. "A single woman interviewing the sex life of a single man. Could hold a lot of intriguing possibilities. Like, what if—"

"The tour?" she reminded him, to get his mind off that train of thought fast.

"Of course, the tour, Professor," he said, very mannerly but obviously getting a kick out of all this.

But no matter how much she tried, Rachel could barely concentrate on his house. In his spacious hi-tech kitchen, sunlit breakfast area, elegant dining room, floor-to-ceiling library of books, and movie screening room, she saw only Zane.

Because Zane Farrell didn't seem like a man she'd just met. She felt as if she'd known him for aeons.

"What do you think of the gym?" Zane asked, breaking into her reverie.

The shiny hardwood-floor gym had blue floor mats, weight machines, treadmills, StairMasters, rowing machines, barbells, and stationary bicycles. Small red dumbbells were carelessly strewn on the floor, and she had to sidestep a couple to avoid tripping.

"This place is bigger than my local health club," she commented.

"It's unreal, isn't it?" he agreed.

"You sound like an amazed visitor rather than the owner of this place," she noted.

"Can't I appreciate the exquisite sight in front of me?" He was gazing straight at her, as if she was the only sight he was aware of.

She nervously clutched her briefcase and stared down at the gym equipment. For a second, she fantasized Zane, half-naked, working up a heated sweat with his muscles bulging as he lifted the heavy weights.

"Professor, I suppose you're viewing this gym in a sexual way," he said.

"N-not exactly." Her cheeks flamed, thinking he had lasered into her fantasies.

"Really?" he went on. "I thought you experts say exercise increases sexual endurance." The roguish glint in his eye made her realize that he was still having fun with her interview. He wasn't treating it seriously at all.

"Is the need for sexual endurance the reason *you* pump iron?" she asked, her chin up for battle.

For a split second, she thought she saw him wince at her insinuation. She wished the words hadn't come out of her mouth so fast.

He tilted his head to one side. "Professor, my *pumping* is not restricted to bars of metal." He kiddingly winked at her for emphasis.

Suddenly furious that he was ridiculing her sex research, she quickly stepped back to exit the gym when her foot stumbled over a dumbbell.

"Ohhhhh!" she screamed as she felt herself go flying.

"Rachel!" Zane called out.

Just then, his powerful hands circled her waist and lifted her. With her feet off the ground, she clutched his strapping upper arms to steady herself, feeling the forceful, protective strength of him.

Zane's firm broad fingers were gripping her body just below her breasts. His large thumbs were pressed up against each swell. Suddenly her nipples ached to be squeezed and fondled by him.

Zane's face was so near she could smell his warm minty breath. His marine eyes focused on her lips.

Her heart jolted, and her pulse pounded. More than anything, she wanted him to kiss her.

She could feel his breath quickening. The muscles of his arms tensed under her palms as he pulled her closer to his hard body. His mouth edged toward hers, and her lips impulsively moved to his.

But as his lips grazed hers, she abruptly became conscious of her unethical behavior. What was she doing? She was a representative of the university, but she was acting like a foolish woman mesmerized by a very sexy man.

Rachel immediately freed herself from Zane's sturdy grasp and set both feet back on the floor. Maybe she shouldn't have allowed two years to go by without being with a man. Maybe all her pent-up sexual energy was suddenly letting loose on the very masculine Zane Farrell.

She avoided his confused eyes, feeling embarrassed and ashamed. She grabbed her fallen briefcase and smoothed down her dress, which had risen to her bare thighs.

"This entire interview has been a big joke to you, hasn't it, Mr. Farrell?" she blurted.

His jaw muscles tensed, momentarily stung by her words. "Is that what you think?"

"Darn right!"

"Am I supposed to act like Joe Serious while you're questioning my virility?" he shot back. "You've been peering at me like I'm some guinea pig for sexual dissection."

Her eyes widened in red fury. "Then why did you volunteer for the study?"

"I obviously made a tremendous mistake, didn't I?"

"Are you saying you're withdrawing your name from this research project?" Her voice was so high-pitched she could barely recognize it. "Because if you are, go right ahead!"

"Fine, Professor Lady!" He abruptly turned to lead her downstairs straight to the double copper doors.

Her hands were sweating against her leather briefcase handle as she hurried after him. What was she saying? She couldn't afford to lose her first case study. The university's administration would surely contact him to ask why he'd dropped out of their research project. He'd inevitably tell them that she'd completely ravaged the interview. She couldn't let him ruin her very first research project!

She bit back her pride for one torturous moment.

"Can't we discuss this matter more calmly, Mr. Farrell?" she asked, searching for the right words to get him back on track with the study.

"*Zane,*" he corrected as he stopped walking and faced her.

"*Mr.* Farrell," she deliberately stressed.

His sparkling blue eyes grew wide with sudden amusement. Then he threw back his head and roared with laughter.

"What's so funny?" She impatiently tapped her foot on the floor. Any second, she was out of there, any second.

"Come on, admit it. You still want me to participate in your research. Yet you refuse to acknowledge that we've just gotten past phase one."

"Phase one?" she repeated, glaring at him from the corner of her eyes in defiant confusion.

"The formalities. The awkwardness. The prim-and-proper front you've put on since you walked through the door."

"That's it!" she howled. "I'm gone!"

She almost dropped her briefcase in her scurrying to grab the door handle. Forget impressing the university administration. She would not be insulted by this gargantuan man!

She rushed out of his house, almost tripped on one of the porch steps, but finally made it to her Valiant. She had to get away from him—far, far away. But her driver's door was stuck, and she couldn't get it open.

"I hate this old car!" she bellowed as she unsuccessfully tugged and tugged to release the door.

Suddenly, Zane was beside her wanting to help. The heat of his body only inches away radiated against hers.

"Don't try so hard, Rachel," he whispered as if he was talking more about the interview than the car door.

With a click and a turn, he unlocked the driver's door with great ease, which further infuriated her. He was about to politely hold it open for her, but she pushed past him into the car.

"*Thank* you," she seethed as she slammed the door closed. Her face felt so hot with anger she felt ready to burst like a balloon.

She started up her Valiant. It belched out a cloud of charcoal smoke that practically surrounded her entire car.

"Professor, your car is screaming for an oil lube," Zane called out. "I can recommend an excellent mechanic—"

"No way!" she cut in, needing badly to get back to State University, her apartment, the Los Angeles Zoo, anywhere but near Zane Farrell!

Two

─────

The moment Rachel's car zoomed away, he rushed back up the stairs to the master suite. He threw off his clean duds and grabbed his oil-stained coveralls and work shirt.

Johnny Wells never meant to fool Rachel Smith. But he had no other choice.

He rushed out of the mansion to Mr. Farrell's four-car garage. His faded maroon pickup truck looked incongruous parked next to Mr. Farrell's emerald Jaguar, sparkling black Mercedes and red Porsche sports car.

The heavy metal door to Johnny's old pickup squeaked as he slammed it closed. He glanced at his callused hands on the steering wheel. Dammit! Black grease was still embedded underneath his fingernails. Had Rachel noticed?

The real Zane Farrell had immaculately clean hands. He'd never had to pick up a wrench or hammer. Why should he? Mr. Farrell could afford to pay workers to do the manual labor for him. Workers like Johnny Wells.

Johnny pressed his boot down harder on the gas pedal as he drove along the curvy narrow roads of Bel Air. His hands perspired on the hot steering wheel. Had Rachel guessed that he wasn't Zane Farrell? He'd really messed up with the Yale thing. He knew zip about master's or miss's degrees.

The last thing Johnny wanted was to screw it up for Mr. Farrell. He highly respected the man. And when he'd agreed to house-sit for Mr. Farrell, Johnny had also made a special promise to him—a promise he didn't dare go back on.

As he zipped his truck out of the exclusive community of Bel Air, he took a deep satisfying breath of normal workingman air. No way did he feel comfortable in posh surroundings. Sure, it was a blast playing the role of a multibillionaire. He didn't mind playacting as Mr. Farrell with the real estate broker who'd come to the mansion door, or the homeowners' insurance guy who'd come by for an appointment Mr. Farrell had forgotten. He'd proudly pulled off both encounters without a glitch.

But for some mysterious reason, his gut burned like a blazing fire, knowing he'd lied to Professor Rachel Smith.

To Johnny, telling the truth was synonymous with being a solid honorable human being. And with Rachel, pretending to be Zane Farrell somehow felt low and dirty.

Johnny jammed on his brakes for a red light on Sunset Boulevard. He was right next to the university campus where Rachel worked.

Johnny felt a slow grin lighten his face. Rachel Smith was definitely not the professor he'd imagined she would be.

On the phone with her, he'd envisioned a high-nosed academic with an uppity attitude, stiff demeanor and brisk manner. But the second he'd yanked open Mr. Farrell's front door to greet her, he'd smelled intoxicating gardenia perfume in the air.

Rachel's soft velvet-brown eyes made him want to stargaze forever. Her silken chestnut hair was pulled tight in a bun, and he'd ached to release her tresses and run his fingers through the smooth strands.

He'd immediately sensed a soft vulnerability about her and felt the instant urge to hold her protectively in his arms.

When she'd spoken about the sexuality study, his gaze was trained to lips which were like flaming red rosebuds ready to be parted with his kiss.

A blaring car horn awakened Johnny to the now-green light on Sunset Boulevard.

He bitterly laughed to himself. Why fool himself? He was definitely no match for Professor Rachel Smith. Once she knew who he really was, she'd immediately take a rocket flight to Venus to get clear of him.

Rachel was from a universe of higher education, renowned books of literature, knowledge of calculus and scientific theories, the privileged world of the scholarly. Zane Farrell's cosmos. But Johnny Wells? He didn't even graduate from high school.

He angrily pushed down the accelerator for a sharp curve. His tires made a screech as if in protest to who he really was.

Why did Mr. Farrell have to volunteer for that sex study, anyway? Johnny had no idea what the man's sexual attitudes were. He certainly didn't want to make him sound like a fizzled dud in bed. Yet, he couldn't portray him as a worldly stud, either. He had to find an acceptable sexual image for the man.

Because Johnny owed Mr. Farrell. He owed him big-time. If it wasn't for Mr. Farrell, Johnny would have remained a runaway teenager on the streets of Los Angeles and maybe ended up with a nowhere life.

It was Mr. Farrell, through his chauffeur, George, who found him on the streets and placed him in a private group home for teens. It was Mr. Farrell who had George enroll Johnny in an auto mechanic's course to professionally learn the kind of work Johnny felt natural doing.

It was Mr. Farrell who had put up the money for a loan for the automotive repair shop that Johnny had dreamed of owning, though Johnny had fought the idea the whole way. He wasn't one to take from anybody, especially someone like Mr. Farrell, whom he'd never even met.

When Johnny requested to meet Mr. Farrell face-to-face, George had immediately told him no. He said Mr. Farrell avoided direct contact with everyone. He refused all social invitations. He lived in total isolation. He never left the grounds of his huge mansion except when he traveled alone. And he would only communicate with Johnny through George.

Johnny tried to figure the man out. He couldn't understand why an eccentric person like Mr. Farrell would shed such kindness upon him. When he asked George, he learned that Mr. Farrell's only son had had a bad drug problem, and one night during a drug deal, he was fatally shot in the head. His son's brutal death had devastated Mr. Farrell. Divorced and alone, Mr. Farrell had spotted Johnny as a runaway teen, and George said that Mr. Farrell wanted to give to Johnny what he'd neglected to give his own son.

Johnny vowed to pay back Mr. Farrell every cent and more. Unbeknownst to Mr. Farrell, Johnny even kept a secret bank account with hard-earned money he was saving to pay back his benefactor for every favor Mr. Farrell had ever done for him. Yes, Johnny owed Mr. Farrell, and he'd never let the man down, not ever.

So when Mr. Farrell asked him over the phone to house-sit while he went on a relaxing worldwide tour, Johnny immediately said yes. And when Mr. Farrell indicated that he'd also given his entire personal staff a vacation but didn't want any corporate competitors to know he was gone, Johnny said he'd make sure even the president didn't know he was away.

But Mr. Farrell had another idea. He asked that Johnny "be him" during any unfinished business he'd forgotten before leaving the country. Even though Johnny wasn't sure if he could pull it off, he didn't hesitate to accept Mr. Farrell's request. Especially when Mr. Farrell told Johnny that he considered him "family" and trusted him implicitly to make all the right business decisions for him.

Johnny steered his pickup into the small parking lot of his shop. His chest expanded with pride as his sign came into view, Johnny's Foreign Automotive Repairs. He loved the black grease of that place, the oil smell, the grime. It was his business, his power in the world.

"Yo, Johnny baby!" called out Tito, his South American mechanic. Tito ran toward Johnny with a face smeared with car oil.

"Tito, any problems while I was gone?" Johnny asked as he turned off his engine. Loyal Tito had been with him from the start.

"You just missed a call from Mr. Farrell," Tito told him with a Spanish accent.

"Man, oh, man, where the hell's my luck?" Johnny bellowed, running frustrated fingers through his curly hair. "I've got to talk to him. He's got me involved in a sex study." Johnny gave Tito a quick rundown on the university project.

"Maybe you should not have made that promise to Mr. Farrell," Tito remarked.

"Tito, I had to—"

"But you have never met the man, Johnny," Tito cut in. "Sure, he helped you in life, but why has he not allowed you to see him? He either talks to you on the phone or through George. He does his business on a computer notebook, cellular phone or through his communications people. Nobody knows who the man is."

"I know him, Tito," Johnny said without a doubt in his head. "He's a private man. He has no wife and no kids to depend on. And he asked me to do him a big favor. And I'm going to do it, Tito, no matter what."

"But how can you, Johnny, when you are not him?" Tito shook his head with confusion.

"I can do it, Tito," Johnny said. "Mr. Farrell's never revealed his age to anyone. Nobody's ever seen his face—"

"Someone will discover you are not Mr. Farrell," Tito cut in. "Somebody you do not want to find out."

Johnny immediately thought of Professor Rachel Smith. She was the only one he was worried about. He didn't like pretending with her. He felt a connection with her, an inner link he'd never felt with any woman before. That's why he was so frustrated that he'd missed Mr. Farrell's phone call. He had to talk to him about that sex test.

Rachel quickened her towel strokes as she dried the dinner dishes in Kim's kitchen. "Kim, I'm taking Zane Farrell's name off the sex-study list."

"You can't do that, Rachel," Kim said, rushing from the sink to clean up her two-year-old daughter, Stacy's, spilled milk on the floor.

A waterfall of tears started streaming down Stacy's chubby cheeks at her mistake. Rachel ran over and lifted the little girl out of the high chair into her arms to soothe her.

"Hey, little one, sometimes I'm a gooky mess, too." Rachel wiggled her finger into Stacy's tummy to make her giggle. "I don't know what I'd do without you, little one." A warm feeling of family enveloped her.

"Stacy would be lost without her second mommy," Kim said with a wink.

Rachel set a now-contented Stacy back in her high chair. She gently kissed Stacy's cheek, but inside, she felt in turmoil. All because of Zane Farrell.

Warmth enveloped her just thinking about his twinkling sea-blue eyes. How he'd sensed the pain inside her when he'd asked her whether sex with a man made her forget who she was. How he'd quickly changed the subject to protect her feelings, even though he didn't understand what they were.

She remembered how her breasts ached to be caressed by him when he'd lifted her in his strong arms in his gym to stop her from falling. And how she'd never wanted him to let go. No, she couldn't go back there, not ever.

"What do you mean, I can't eliminate Farrell from the study?" Rachel prompted. "He's not right for the research. We'll find another entrepreneur for the upper-crust category."

"No, we won't," her friend said firmly. "Unless you want to buck heads with Chancellor Zilford."

"The chancellor?" A ripple of nervousness flitted through her. More than anything, she wanted to impress the head of the university with her first research assignment.

"When Chancellor Zilford heard that Zane Farrell had volunteered for the study, he gave his hundred-percent approval to the project."

"Why?" She suddenly felt Kim's delicious chicken-cutlet dinner nauseatingly rise in her throat.

"Before you came to the university, Zane Farrell donated three million for a new building on campus. The chancellor plans to name the structure Farrell Hall. I don't think he would appreciate learning you scratched Mr. Farrell's name from the research list."

"But I can't work with him," she protested, feeling helpless. "He's a thick-headed, overgrown—"

"Are you talking about me?" asked Kim's husband, Charlie, as he sauntered into the kitchen munching on a fire-engine-red apple.

"Maybe we are, handsome," Kim teased as she lifted Stacy out of her high chair, patted the little girl's cute behind and sent her off to the living room to play.

Charlie slipped his arms around his wife's waist and planted a deep kiss on her mouth.

"Am I impossible now?" he murmured against Kim's ear.

Rachel felt an ache in her heart and turned back to drying the dishes. She both admired and envied Kim's marriage of six years. She knew a forever-love like theirs could never happen to her. Not after the catastrophe that had occurred between her and Kent two years ago.

Her eyes blurred as the nightmare evening flashed into her mind. Three days before their wedding, she and Kent were kissing on his apartment sofa. She'd known him since junior high and had never gone out with any other man.

But on that fateful night as Rachel pressed her eager body to his and parted her lips against his mouth, Kent abruptly pulled away. He got off the sofa and paced the floor, avoiding her confused eyes.

"Kent, what's wrong?" she asked. "What did I do?"

Then Kent let loose in a way that would mar her life from that moment on.

"Do you know why we've never had intercourse together?" he blasted.

"Because we want to wait for our wedding night," she replied, feeling a chill as an ice wall grew between them.

"No!" he blurted out. "It's because I don't want to make love to you, Rachel." His face twisted in agony, looking shocked by his own admission.

"Wh-what do you mean?" she stammered, clutching the neckline of her blouse together, as if to shield her exposed heart from him.

"You're always thinking about sex," he said tightly. "You're always touching me. Always so easily aroused. With your heavy breathing and excessive bodily reactions, you're downright intimidating."

"Kent, don't say that," she cried out. He was tearing apart her soul.

"You make me feel sexually inadequate," he railed. "No man will ever be able to satisfy you, Rachel. No man."

In Kim's kitchen, Rachel flopped down on a chair at the table. She was still reeling from Kent's accusations. Two whole years wasn't enough time for her to recover from his verbal attack on her sexuality. From that moment on, she'd closed herself off from all sexual feeling, all sexual fantasies and any deep emotional affinity she could ever share with a man. Until Zane Farrell.

That's why she couldn't see Zane again. He'd unlocked her Pandora's box. He'd touched the most bruised and vulnerable spot of her entire being. He'd connected with her heart.

Kim gave Charlie another peck on the lips. "Now get out of here, Charlie Woods." She playfully pushed him into the living room to his daughter and then turned to Rachel.

"Take my advice," Kim urged. "If you want to stay in good with the chancellor, you better give Zane Farrell one more chance."

"Kim, I can't," she said in a desperate tone. "Will you take over his interviews for me?"

"I wish I could," Kim replied. "But my schedule's horribly tight right now. Rachel, I don't understand. Why are you so anxious to get rid of Farrell?"

"The man's totally impossible," she said, avoiding Kim's eyes.

She could feel Kim studying her in that close-girlfriend way of hers. "Rachel, are you attracted to him?"

"Definitely *not!*" she denied. Her friend's knowing hazel eyes were still on her. "Okay, okay, the man *is* sort of sexy."

"Sort of?"

"He's a major turn-on."

"And you want to give him up?"

"I don't need a member of the male population in my life right now, Kim."

"What are you afraid of, Rachel?" Kim asked with concern. "It's still Kent, isn't it?"

"No!" she insisted, unable to summon the courage to tell her friend the horror of shame she felt about her sexual self.

"Please, Kim, will you take the Zane Farrell case study from me?" she begged. "I still have the accountant and orthopedic surgeon to interview. No one will even notice."

Kim was silent as she poured them both a cup of herbal tea. "As soon as my schedule frees up, I'll take Farrell from you. Can you hold out until then?"

"You promise?" Rachel asked, praying she really would.

"Promise."

Rachel hugged her. "I owe you, buddy."

All day at his car-repair shop, that university sex study Mr. Farrell had volunteered for was busting Johnny's brains. He dreaded telling Mr. Farrell that he'd totally messed up the interview. But he was going to admit it, nonetheless.

"Tito, did Mr. Farrell say when he'd call me back?" Johnny asked as he handed a customer her car key after completing her repairs.

"Mr. Farrell said he was going to Taiwan," Tito responded.

"Did he leave a phone number where I can reach him?"

"No number, Johnny," Tito replied. "He told me he is sure you are handling everything A-OK for him. He is not worried. He knows you will make all the correct decisions in his place."

"Riiigght," Johnny slurred under his breath. "Thanks, Tito."

"One more thing, Johnny," Tito added, rubbing his nose with an oily hand and smudging more lubricant on his face. "My lady asked if you will come over and eat with us. She will make your favorite *chalupa*."

"Name the date and time and I'll be there," Johnny replied, a smile coming to his face at just the thought.

Tito's wife and four kids had taken him in like one of their own. Johnny's mother and father were killed in an auto accident when he was twelve years old. Their car brakes had faltered. He ran away from the abusive Michigan foster home he was put in, and hitchhiked to Los Angeles where Mr. Farrell found him and guided him back to constructive living. Maybe Johnny's parents' car tragedy was the reason that keeping automobiles in perfect order was so important to him.

It was closing time, but three cars in need of repair pulled into Johnny's shop, anyway. He could never refuse a customer who needed service. His shop was suddenly spinning with malfunctioning Volvos and M.G.'s. He barely had time to think about Rachel Smith and her sex interview.

That is, until later that evening. Johnny spent one night a week in his own apartment while house-sitting for Mr. Farrell. As Johnny watered the miniature vegetable garden he'd planted on the small plot beside his rent-controlled Santa Monica apartment, his mind wandered to Professor Rachel Smith.

Maybe it was the silver moon in the black velvet sky. Maybe he was tired and his body was beginning to relax. But as he sprayed his tomato plants, Johnny fantasized that Rachel was standing in front of him right that moment. He wanted to bask in the warmth of her feminine presence and delight in her defiant, stubborn and exciting nature.

He pictured Rachel's swelling ivory breasts spilling over her spaghetti-strapped rose-colored dress as he'd gripped her waist in Mr. Farrell's gym.

When her taut nipples strained against the cotton fabric, he'd realized her ample breasts were bra-free. How close his hungry mouth had been to suckling one pert nipple.

The sprinkling garden hose suddenly veered off course into his landlord's cactus plant. He quickly turned off the water faucet. In a few minutes, he hit the bed, still smelling the sweet gardenia scent of her skin.

He fisted his pillow several times to get comfortable, but he was plagued with Rachel Smith thoughts. He kept picturing her soft body cuddled up to his in a tender embrace.

Restless, he got up and peered out the window at the shining star-glazed night. A half smile formed on his lips. Rachel had practically stripped her car gears to get away from him.

Yes, he'd definitely ticked her off. He'd gotten to her academic insides and stirred her up a bit. She was highly emotional, he could tell. Women who got that stormy, that quickly, usually had a healthy passionate nature and a tender sensitivity. He couldn't deny it. He was irresistibly drawn to Rachel, more than to any woman he'd ever known.

A cloud suddenly hid the moon, and a dark shadow brushed over Johnny's heart. *Forget your emotional pull to Rachel,* he silently told himself. *You're invisible to her. She sees Zane Farrell, not you.*

He'd permitted his own powerful attraction to her to seep through and go beyond the boundary he had to have with Professor Smith. He wouldn't let that happen again. No sir. He wasn't going to disappoint Mr. Farrell.

He had to make Mr. Farrell's volunteer study a successful one. Not that Johnny could figure out why a man like Mr. Farrell would ever participate in a sex research project.

Johnny hopped back into bed and punched his pillow into a snug position. Professor Rachel Smith, get ready. Mr. Farrell's sex study was definitely not over yet. Johnny would play his role with more of a Zane Farrell cultured flare and not allow the uncouth, uneducated Johnny Wells to interfere again.

The next morning, Rachel pressed the fifteenth-floor elevator button in the steel-and-glass building in downtown Los Angeles for her second case-study interview, Harvey Glitt, a certified public accountant to the wealthiest business people in Los Angeles.

In the accounting office, Rachel tried to concentrate on quiet, shy Harvey Glitt with his bow tie, tall bony frame and pale complexion. Harvey yearned for a relationship with a woman, almost begged for one. The poor man had negative sex appeal. Maybe he was the type of male she needed. No arousal threat. Only platonic friends.

Rachel knew if she ever let loose her sexuality again with Zane Farrell, she'd lose her sensibilities, her logic, and would end up in a disastrous situation like the one she'd been in with Kent. And she never wanted to hurt Zane that way.

She made an unending vow to herself. The next time she was with Zane, she would demolish every emotionally close and sensually tempting thought that rose to her consciousness. Zane would remain a purely academic study to her. That was all.

The moment she returned to her office at the university, she quickly recovered Zane Farrell's home phone number from the trash can where she'd angrily hurled it after their last encounter.

She nervously fingered the wrinkled sheet of paper. Excuses for never seeing him again lightning-flashed through her mind. But she refused to retreat. She'd keep it friendly but emotionally distant.

Just as she picked up the phone, there was a knock at her closed office door. She barely uttered a "come in" when the door powerfully swung open Zane Farrell–style. A bouquet of gleaming white gardenias were in Zane's hands.

"Rachel, before you throw a lamp at me," he began in his deeply resonating voice, "can we make a truce?" He handed her the sweetly scented flowers and added, "The aroma is definitely you."

Rachel was so surprised, she couldn't utter a word. She hugged the precious gardenias to her and inhaled a long, deep intake of flower-scented air with her eyes never leaving his.

Zane leaned against the wall of her office watching her, as if he belonged, like he was part of her life. And for that second, she wished that he really was.

Stop it, Rachel Smith. Control yourself. You promised.

She set the flowers down on her desk. "I assume this is a confirmation that you're still a candidate for the university study?" she managed to say in her best businesslike voice.

"Only if you'll have dinner with me tonight at The Wave Restaurant."

His enticing eyes twinkled at her, and she suspected that his invitation was filled with much more than thoughts of the case study.

Thump, thump, thump, went her heart. A romantic dinner. Tenderly holding hands at the table. Eyes entwined. An invitation back to his mansion. Then a peak at his bedroom. Then his bed.

Be the professor, not the woman, she cautioned herself.

"Will the restaurant be conducive for our interview?" she asked carefully.

"Absolutely. One hundred percent," he said confidently. "Eight o'clock?"

"Seven," she firmly countered.

He chuckled as though pleased she was still wearing her battle gear. "Seven it is, Professor Smith. Shall I pick you up here or at your apartment?"

"I'll meet you at the restaurant." Keep it impersonal. Distant. All business.

"I look forward to it." Then he was gone.

She plopped down on her desk chair. Why did he have to touch her heart by bringing those beautiful flowers? And why did he have to be so sexy? Could he see her trembling in his presence?

She quickly phoned Kim for support. "Kim, I can't go to dinner with him," she said, nervously stretching the phone cord.

"Just concentrate on the study," Kim advised.

"How soon will you be freed up to take over his interviews?"

"Maybe in a week or so." Her friend hesitated. "Will you be okay?"

"As long as I can see an end to it," she replied. Her mind felt partially at ease as she hung up the phone. Knowing her stint with Zane Farrell was short-lived, she'd be just fine.

The black-tied maître d' approached Rachel as she entered The Wave Restaurant in Beverly Hills. The round tables were covered with mauve tablecloths and butterfly-folded napkins. Elegant black candles flickered on the tables like diamonds.

She hoped she hadn't underdressed. Women were in sparkling sequins. Men in suave Italian suits.

Rachel had deliberately worn a beige silk blouse with lacy collar and sleeves and a form-fitting maroon skirt. Her hair was softly up in a bun with a wisp of bangs over her forehead. She felt conservatively businesslike, which was exactly the impression she wanted to give Zane Farrell.

As she followed the maître d', her breath caught in her throat. Zane arose from his table at the sight of her. A pinstriped black suit covered his muscular frame. His luminous blue eyes were focused on her as though she were the only woman in the galaxy.

Keep cool, girl, keep cool.

"Rachel," Zane whispered as he gently took her hand in his warm palm. "You look lovely."

"Thank you," she replied, quickly slipping free of his electrically charged touch. *Keep him physically away,* she warned herself. *Stay in one emotional piece.*

Johnny couldn't take his eyes off her. How could her face radiate more beauty than any female he'd ever met? She was even more gorgeous than the last time he'd seen her.

His focus slipped to her silken top, which feathered across her ample curves as she moved. The fabric was so fine that a trace of lacy bra peeked through. He could see a hint of her bountiful breasts puffing over the top of her lingerie.

He swallowed as he pulled out her chair. When she sat down, her skirt rose to the tops of her luscious bare thighs. She wasn't wearing any stockings. His breathing quickened. He rapidly took his own seat before she caught him staring like a teenage boy.

Johnny had found The Wave Restaurant listed as one of Beverly Hills' finest eateries. Since Mr. Farrell ordered in all meals to his mansion and never appeared in restaurants, Johnny didn't worry about using the man's name.

"About the incident in your gym," Rachel began. "It shouldn't have happened."

"Why not?" Johnny asked.

"It was improper," she replied.

"*Im*proper?" Johnny repeated with a chuckle. "Come on, Rachel. The gym thing happened because you and I are very attracted to each other. Why can't you admit—"

Johnny stopped when he saw the shocked look on Rachel's face. He wanted to punch himself in the gut. Mr. Farrell was never coarse. But Johnny Wells was street-rough through and through.

"My focus is *strictly* on this research project," Rachel said, looking him straight in the eyes. "Not on you."

Rachel thought she saw Zane flinch. But she couldn't let herself care. She had to keep the concrete wall up to protect herself from this man who possessed the power to bring out the achingly vulnerable part of herself that she vowed to keep concealed forever.

"Hey, no problem," Zane told her, his voice dropping. He leaned back in his cushioned seat. "I'll answer any question you ask. With one stipulation."

"What's that?"

"For every sex question you ask me, you have to respond to one of mine."

"No," she quickly said. "It wouldn't be appropriate."

"Why not?" he asked. "You're bold enough to probe my male psyche. Why can't I explore the sex fantasies floating around in yours?"

Rachel immediately gulped down a long sip of sparkling water from the crystal glass. She couldn't possibly accept his proposal. She couldn't tell him her sexual thoughts. She couldn't tell anyone. Yet, she had to make sure that Zane Farrell didn't back out of the study. The chancellor's potential upset threateningly stared her in the face.

"If you *insist* on mutual questioning," she began in a strained voice, "I'll go along with it. But if I don't feel like answering, you bet I won't."

"Same here," he said with a pleased grin that made her even more nervous about the whole matter. "Kick off the text."

Just then, to her utter relief, the waiter brought their dinners. Zane ate his shrimp scampi with a conspicuous appetite. She barely took a bite of hers. She didn't know how to begin her sex questions. As the dinner neared its end and she anxiously fiddled with her chocolate mousse, she noticed Zane placing a final forkful of creamy mousse into his mouth.

She caught a glimpse of his tongue licking off some excess chocolate on the fork. The sensitive area between her legs woke up. The thought of his mouth on her throbbing breasts—

Stop it! she silently scolded herself.

She struggled to ignore the arousing sensations sizzling through her body and pulled out the questionnaire folder from her briefcase. She stared at the first question. *Oh, no, I can't ask that one!* she silently screamed. *Don't think about it. Just blurt it out.*

"How often do you self-pleasure?" she managed to say, glancing away from his uplifted eyebrow.

"Play with my—"

"Masturbate," she choked out. He was enjoying this. She was sure of it.

"You're assuming that I do."

"Don't you?" she asked, a slow burn rushing to her cheeks.

"Do you?" he curiously inquired.

Johnny watched the skin on Rachel's stunning face turn ashen. He didn't mean to embarrass her. Yet, wasn't that what she was doing to him? Was the masturbation question acceptable only if she asked it?

He noticed her nervously biting her lower lip, and for a moment, he hated that he'd probed. He impulsively touched her soft hand with his rough callused one.

"Hey, forget it, Rachel," Johnny said. "You want to go for a ride in Mr. Fa—my Porsche?"

"Sure," she whispered.

Johnny noticed that Rachel's hands were trembling as she stuck the questionnaire back in her briefcase. He got up from his chair feeling confused. Something just didn't click for him. Why would an academic doing a sexuality study be afraid to talk about sex herself?

When she rose from her seat, her briefcase slipped to the floor and papers spewed out. Johnny bent down to help her. As she crouched, he noticed her maroon skirt skidding up her naked thighs. Her bare legs spread slightly.

He sucked in his breath at the glimpse of pink lace panties covering the feminine mound between her velvety thighs. He wanted to press his hand intimately against the pink expanse and—

What the hell was he thinking? He shoved the loose papers into her briefcase and got to his feet. He was supposed to be acting like well-mannered Zane Farrell, not some lewd male with a hanging tongue.

The summer evening wind in the racing red Porsche convertible was undoing a part of Rachel's bun. She grabbed the flying strands.

"Want the top up?" Johnny called above the whir of the freeway. Her hair was wildly blowing around her face. He imagined that was the uninhibited way she looked while making love.

"I'm fine!" Rachel yelled back as she struggled to get her hair into place.

She hadn't been able to look Zane in the eyes since leaving the restaurant.

How could she tell him that, yes, she loved the titillating sensations she could create in her own body. And, yes, she had caressed her private areas many, many times before drifting to sleep at night.

But she didn't dare. Because when she'd revealed her private moments to her about-to-be husband, Kent, months before their wedding, he'd stared at her in utter shock. He'd accused her of being sexually selfish and disturbingly obsessed with her own physical pleasure. And every time they were together after that, Kent asked if she'd caressed herself the night before. She was so haunted with guilt and shame that she hadn't intimately touched her own body since.

"Hey, I didn't mean to send you into shock back at the restaurant," Zane shouted over the wind, cutting into her tortured thoughts. "Can I make it up to you by finishing the tour of my house for your interview?"

"I really don't—" Rachel knew she didn't dare return to the intimacy of his house at night. But with the roaring car engine and the wind whisking by, Zane didn't hear her resist.

The Porsche zoomed through his King Kong gate and shot right to the curb in front of the mansion.

As Johnny led Rachel into Mr. Farrell's palace, a twinge of sadness dragged at his heart. He wished he could take her to his small comfortable apartment in Santa Monica. He wanted to show her his vegetable garden. Maybe listen to a jazz CD and sip white wine while lying on pillows together on the floor.

He mentally kicked himself. *Face reality, Johnny boy,* he reprimanded himself. Professor Rachel Smith wouldn't associate with a mediocre-incomed, uneducated engine fixer, even if he did have his own shop.

"Which room did we leave out last time?" Johnny asked as he removed his suit jacket and threw it on the sofa. He had to remind himself that Rachel was here to interview Mr. Farrell, not him. He was going to portray the man in neon colors. Just as long as his own street-level personality didn't push into the frame.

"I believe you neglected to show me the master bedroom," Rachel said. The sex questionnaire required it. But it was the room she most dreaded entering. The suggestive chamber that would surely tempt her wildest fantasies.

She lifted her chin, determined to be strong and not emotionally vulnerable again.

That is, until she hit his luxurious master suite. Her gaze settled on the exotic circular bed. The raven-black satin comforter and creamy vanilla pillows winked at her in greeting.

Zane rubbed a large palm across the softness of the glossy bedspread.

"Cool, huh?" he offered. "What does the bedroom decor say about me?"

"That you've got an excellent interior decorator."

"That's all?" he asked, sounding disappointed.

No, it wasn't all. She envisioned herself tumbling nude with Zane into all that milky, silky satin.

She fought her fantasies and fumbled in her briefcase for her pad and pencil.

"Why did you choose a round bed?" she managed to ask as she steadied her quivering fingers to write.

Zane sat on the bed and patted the spot beside him, beckoning her to him.

"Why don't you find out for yourself?" he suggested in a velvet murmur.

"I'd rather hear your thoughts on it," she stated in a professorial voice. "I may interpret your bedroom accoutrements quite differently from the actual reason you purchased them. After all, what is sexy is purely subjective, isn't it?"

"You tell me. You're the lovemaking expert."

His intense gaze caught and held hers. She was superaware of being alone with him in his bedroom. Super-aware of the closeness she felt toward him. Super-aware of his circular satiny bed and wanting to make love with him.

Zane arose from the bed and approached her. "Are you afraid of me, Rachel?"

"Why should I be?" She struggled to ignore the charged currents shooting from his body to hers. She strained to get his attention off her.

"Is that your master bathroom?" she began, struggling to hold on, fighting to forget the humiliating truth about herself that she never wanted Zane to find out.

She entered the bathroom, which was the size of her entire apartment bedroom. Lavender and gray tiles. Recessed lighting. Gray porcelain Jacuzzi tub.

Her gaze stopped at the spacious clear-glassed shower stall with double chrome shower heads on either side. For two people. Scrubbing down each other's hot dripping bodies. She bit down on her bottom lip.

Johnny followed her into the bathroom and leaned against the glass shower door. She wouldn't even look him in the eyes. What was she hiding from? Had he said or done anything to trouble her? If he had, he'd take it back instantly if he knew what it was.

He could see her breasts heaving under the silk top. He wanted to pull her into his arms and smother his face between the softness of those warm swelling globes.

She fumbled with her questionnaire. "Have you ever taken a shower with a woman?"

"Have you with a man?" Johnny inquired. He had no right to ask, but he couldn't stop himself. He wanted to know every intimate detail about her.

"I asked you first," she insisted.

"I think sharing a shower with a woman can be great foreplay."

"Is that a yes for the study?" she asked.

"Absolutely," he replied. "Have *you*, Rachel?"

"Have I what?"

"Taken a shower with a man."

She nervously flipped through the printed questionnaire without answering.

"You're breaking our agreement," Johnny said.

"No, I'm not."

"I'm baring all to you. Why are you keeping secrets from me?"

"I'm as open as you are."

"Then answer my shower question."

"I have *never* shared a shower. Happy?"

"Not if I was the man in your life."

"Well, you're not!"

"Good!"

"Fine!"

Before she could protest further, Johnny pulled Rachel's trembling body to his. His mouth covered her rosebud lips. He could feel her palms against his chest.

"Rachel," Johnny whispered in a gravelly tone.

His lips nibbled, bit, devoured her mouth, savoring the gardenia flavor of her. He felt her defensive grip slowly loosen on his chest. Then she bit and suckled back. His fingers undid her tight bun. Her silken hair flowed through his palms like a gentle waterfall.

Rachel arched her back in response to Zane's touch. She didn't stop him from pulling her blouse out of the protection of her skirt. His hot hands slid under her top and cupped her lace-covered breasts. She inhaled sharply.

As Zane kneaded and squeezed the flesh filling her bra, a deep guttural groan escaped from the depths of his throat.

Rachel felt her resistance weaken. All of her determined self-control was slowly ebbing. Her eager hands touched up and down Zane's muscular chest, feeling the strained muscles under her palms, feeling his manliness engulf her senses.

Her promise to herself was draining, draining, draining out of her brain. The exhilarating manly taste of him was obliterating, destroying, shattering the iron shield she'd created for two long years.

Three

Rachel parted her lips, allowing Zane's free entry into the intimacy of her mouth. His tongue danced with hers, teasing, tasting, probing, searching. She forgot who she was, where she was.

She spread her hands through his hair, wrapping her fingers around the curls, winding each tighter as fiery radiations peaked and soared through her body.

Her breathing came quickly as she urgently undid the buttons of his shirt, wanting to feel his firm flesh, wanting to get closer to him. She spread his shirt apart, and her eager hands caressed his bulging muscles and wantonly grazed the wiry hair on his hard chest.

A groan escaped from Zane as his mouth hungrily tasted hers. She tilted her head back as his lips nibbled down the crest of her neck. His touch was sensitive, gentle, the way she'd dreamed he'd be. Tingles slithered along the length of her body. His tongue licked her throat, as if he couldn't get enough of the taste of her.

Far, far in the distance, Rachel heard ringing. But her mind and body were reeling, spinning. All that was real to her was getting closer to Zane. It felt so good, so good. The rainbow spasms exploded through her limbs.

Suddenly, the ringing got louder, and she realized it was a phone. Zane slowly released his mouth from hers.

"Rachel, wait," he whispered with glazed blue eyes. "I'll be right back." He momentarily left her and went to answer the phone in the bedroom.

Alone in the bathroom, Rachel caught her reflection in the mirror and stared at it in horror. Her lipstick was smeared. Her hair was undone. Her blouse was in disarray.

Outrage charred every brain cell. She'd shattered her pledge to herself. She'd failed, oh, had she failed.

Her throat tightened as she struggled to tug her blouse inside her skirt with trembling fingers. How could she have let herself unleash the erotic feelings she'd safely hidden away? How could she?

Zane quickly returned to her. "The line went dead before I could answer," he said. His shirt was hanging open from her unbuttoning. His bare chest was exposed where her fingers had wantonly grazed.

Her face flamed with shame. She yanked her hair back into a bun, angry, furious at herself.

"What's the matter?" he asked.

"This is all wrong," she murmured, so embarrassed, so undeniably humiliated by her actions. Zane had seen her grabbing at him, needing, wanting. She wanted to die, just die.

"Wrong?" he repeated, not understanding.

"I'm not here to have an affair with you, Mr. Farrell."

"I didn't intend for this to happen."

"I've got to go." She grabbed her briefcase, which had fallen to the floor in their rush of passion.

"Don't," he said in a raw voice as he gently touched her shoulder.

"I came to do research, Mr. Farrell, not—not—" Her words caught. She furiously rushed past him out of the bathroom.

Johnny angrily slammed his fist against the bathroom door. What the hell was he doing? He'd gone severely past the image he was supposed to present as Mr. Farrell. And hearing Rachel call him Mr. Farrell made him excruciatingly aware that he was one big ugly lie. One immense deceitful personality, and he despised himself for it.

Johnny drove Rachel to get her Valiant, which she'd left parked at The Wave Restaurant. She never once talked to him, never once looked at him.

He tightly clenched his jaw until pain seared across his cheeks. He didn't blame her for hating him. He'd just proven what he knew to be true about himself. He had no class. He didn't come within an inch of the intellectual and social caliber of Zane Farrell. That Rachel still believed he was Mr. Farrell was astounding to him.

She jumped out of the Porsche before he had a chance to open the passenger door for her. He helplessly watched as she got into her car and drove away. She didn't even say goodbye.

Johnny peeled away from the curb so fast he smelled burning rubber. Damn it! Why had he allowed himself to touch her tempting body? He would have made love to her on the bathroom floor if she'd let him. Luckily, she hadn't. He was a phony. A fake. But why did it matter so much to him who she thought he was?

Because Johnny realized Rachel Smith was special. Very special. In an extraordinary way that no woman had ever been to him. He wanted to know her fully, completely, not just sexually, but her mind, her heart, her soul.

Yet, Johnny knew the inevitable fate of his powerful attraction to Rachel. Total doom. Zero destiny together. All because he was not prestigious, intellectual Mr. Zane Farrell. He was Mr. Johnny 'Nobody' Wells.

But he was determined about one thing. He wasn't going to allow Rachel to go on thinking he was somebody he wasn't.

As he raced the red Porsche back to the mansion, he picked up Mr. Farrell's cellular car phone. He was going to reach Zane Farrell if he had to call all over the solar system to find him.

Rachel took two blueberry muffins from the counter at the crowded university cafeteria. She placed one on her tray and the other on Kim's as they sat down at a table.

"Rachel, you're flushed," Kim commented. Then her eyes lit up. "Don't tell me. You were with Zane Farrell last night, weren't you?"

"Yes," she mumbled almost inaudibly. She nibbled on the muffin feeling numb, unable to taste the sweet blueberry inside.

"Did you kiss him?" her friend pursued, wide-eyed, dying to hear the juicy details.

"Kiss him?" Rachel repeated in a panic. The blueberry muffin went tumbling out of her weak fingers onto the linoleum floor. "What—what do you mean?"

Had Zane Farrell called the university to report her unethical behavior? Was her new career destroyed all because she had no sexual control?

"You *did* kiss him," Kim went on. "I knew it!"

"I didn't mean to. I really didn't, Kim."

"Sure you did," Kim said excitedly. "And that's great. You've finally stuck Kent down in the dark cellar. Good for you!"

"You don't understand," she struggled to tell her. "The kiss was a major, major mistake."

"Rachel, if you enjoyed it, so what?"

"Enjoyed it?" Rachel repeated, mortified, covering her face with her hands. Oh, how she absolutely, undeniably loved his full lips devouring hers and the feel of his powerful muscled chest against the palms of her hands. She'd enjoyed his tender, firm touch, and his caring, warm kisses trailing down her neck. She'd have stripped him naked if that phone hadn't rung!

"Don't worry yourself about it," her friend said, picking up the muffin from the floor for her. "Your troubles with Zane Farrell are over."

"Why?" she tensely asked. "Are they taking the research project from me?" Zane *had* called the university. The chancellor knew. Kim was afraid to tell her. A wave of nausea hit her like a typhoon.

"No, no, nothing like that," Kim replied. "My schedule's lightened up. I can take over the Farrell case study for you."

Rachel waited for a sparkling ray of joy to radiate within her. No more frustration with his feisty, bold nature. No more worrying about her untamed passion letting loose. No more concern about the close bond she was forming with him. She was through with Zane Farrell for good.

Then why did a hollow feeling resound deep in the caverns of her soul?

"Don't you hear me?" Kim went on. "You're free of Zane Farrell!"

"Wh-when do you start interviewing him?" she stammered. Her throat felt tight and dry. She wouldn't have to deal with Zane's sea-blue eyes teasing her anymore. She wouldn't feel the erotic intensity of his hands or his mouth on her throbbing skin. She wouldn't feel her heart swelling with warmth knowing he wanted to be with her as much as she wanted to be with him.

"I can take your place immediately," Kim replied.

Abruptly, Rachel got up from the table and put away her tray. Her heart was racing. Her mind felt muddled with confusion.

"Rachel, what's wrong?" her friend asked, following Rachel out of the cafeteria.

Rachel couldn't answer. She didn't know, herself. She quickened her pace on the shaded campus path. The majestic university buildings and swaying green eucalyptus trees surrounded her like a protective natural force.

The scholarly environment took her out of her narrow mental world and made her suddenly aware of the power and prestige of being a professor. She was educating fertile minds. She was researching a paper that would be printed in a university publication for all to ponder for years to come.

"Rachel, admit it," Kim said, trying to keep up with her sprite pace. "You're emotionally stuck on this guy."

"I'm *not* stuck on him," she insisted.

"If you weren't, one little kiss wouldn't matter."

Rachel stopped walking. "It wasn't little."

Kim's eyes beamed with delight. "There! You see? You *are* falling for Zane Farrell, aren't you?"

"Yes, I mean, no, I mean, oh, I'm so mixed up!" Her next words came rushing out before she had time to think them through. "Kim, would you be mad at me if I took back Zane's case study? I want to complete the interviews myself."

"I'd be happy if you did!" Her friend hugged her, said she'd see her later and headed off.

As Rachel walked into the lecture hall, the truth glared at her like a sunlit day. Meeting Zane Farrell had whirled her world around. He was the most wonderful, impressive man she'd ever met. Not only because of the colossal empire he'd built around himself, but because he seemed so unaffected by his royal life-style. That's what attracted her the most. Zane Farrell was a *real* person under that upper-crust facade.

She was determined to call him for another appointment. She'd force herself to forget their succulent kisses and her grabbing at him with such need. She couldn't let her mistakes hold her back from completing her research project.

As Rachel entered the lecture hall, buzzing college students were in their seats waiting for her. A powerful surge of energy shot through her. She watched her students' eyes widen with intellectual curiosity as she began her animated discourse.

Johnny held the shop telephone in his oily hand as he tried reaching Mr. Farrell again. Last night at the mansion, he'd called Taiwan several times but couldn't locate the hotel where Mr. Farrell was staying. It was hard enough finding English-speaking hotel staff to talk to, but the static on Mr. Farrell's silver portable phone didn't help, either. He had to remember to replace the phone battery.

Johnny had made up his mind. He'd tell Mr. Farrell that he'd continue to "be him" in business matters, but not in the university sex study. Not with Professor Rachel Smith. Not with the woman he wanted to be with more than anyone else he knew.

"Hello?" Johnny said into the phone when he heard a voice answer from the last hotel he could find in Taiwan. "Do you have a Mr. Zane Farrell registered? I'm calling for Los Angeles, California, in the United States."

"Ah, yes, sir, we do, sir," the hotel clerk said in very good English. "Mr. Farrell has been here. I believe he placed a long-distance call from the hotel to Los Angeles sometime yesterday. However, no one answered his call."

Damn it! Johnny scolded himself. While Mr. Farrell was trying to reach him at the mansion last night, he was immersed in the lusciousness of Rachel's body. If he'd acted graciously, the way he was supposed to, he'd have received Mr. Farrell's call.

"Is Mr. Farrell available now?" Johnny frantically asked.

"I am sorry, sir, but Mr. Farrell left Taiwan early this morning," the clerk replied. "I believe he is on his way to Cairo."

"Cairo?" Johnny repeated with frustration. "Did he leave a forwarding number?"

"Yes, sir, he did."

Relieved, Johnny immediately phoned the prestigious hotel in Cairo. He was told that Mr. Farrell had registered, but he wasn't in his room. Johnny left a message for him to call Los Angeles right away. He slammed down the phone.

"Johnny, baby, why are your nerves shot this morning?" Tito asked as he entered Johnny's small office. He was holding a rusty muffler.

"Tito, have you ever known a woman who was so irresistible you couldn't keep your hands off her?" Johnny asked, feeling comfortable talking about females with Tito. Tito had been around the planet a few more times than Johnny.

"Yeah, I know one woman just like that." Tito beamed. "That's why I married her."

"You're a lucky man, Tito," he said.

Johnny sifted through some bills on his grimy desk not really seeing the print in front of him. Tito and his wife were baked from the same dough. Not like him and Rachel. She'd end up with a tenured professor at the university. A man of the intelligentsia who could expound on the analytical intricacies of Darwin and Aristotle. But Johnny Wells? She'd laugh right in his greasy face.

"Johnny, who is this woman that makes your heart flame?"

"No, no, Tito," Johnny quickly protested, protective of his strong feelings for Rachel, knowing she could never return them. "My heart is *not* the part she sets on fire."

Tito chuckled knowingly. "I see. I see."

"She's a professor doing some business with Mr. Farrell," he explained, his voice suddenly dropping.

Tito didn't miss it. "She thinks you are him?"

"Exactly."

"If your heart is not involved, then there is no problem, right?"

"Correct."

"But that is not the case."

Johnny was about to deny it, but the all-knowing gaze of Tito persuaded him not to. No matter what words Johnny used, Tito lasered into the truth behind them.

"Tito, she's incredibly intelligent," Johnny began. "A university scholar. And she's vivacious and gorgeous and she—"

"Does not know you are Johnny Wells," Tito finished sadly, hopelessly shaking his head. "You are sunk, Johnny baby. You are not the person she sees. You must detach yourself from that ravishing female. Or else, you are in for much pain."

"I know, Tito, I know," Johnny said. Tito had hit the lotto number. Falling for Rachel was disaster time. Her attraction was not for him but for the prestigious name and social status of powerful mogul Mr. Zane Farrell—her intellectual equal.

The ringing of the shop telephone abruptly sliced into Johnny's misery. Tito quickly answered it.

"It is Mrs. Guillino," Tito told him. "She has bad car trouble at Will Rogers State Park. Can you tow her back to the shop?"

"I'm already there." Johnny immediately hopped into his tow truck.

Mrs. Guillino was a loyal customer. She regularly brought in her red Jaguar convertible and her husband's DeLorean. Mr. Guillino owned a string of supermarkets in Southern California. She was class and so was he. A perfect duo. Another confirmation that opposites like him and Rachel were doomed.

Johnny's tow truck barreled up Sunset Boulevard. As he passed the university, his heart hammered against his rib cage. He remembered the gardenia flavor in his mouth when he'd kissed Rachel. How her hands had intimately touched his chest. How close he'd felt to her. And how her eager body had pressed against his.

He shifted uncomfortably in his tow-truck seat. His bodily equipment actively responded inside his coveralls.

Johnny reached the parking lot of Will Rogers State Park. He immediately sighted Mrs. Guillino's red Jag. But she was nowhere around. He walked toward the main park building. As he reached the entry door, he froze in his tracks.

Off in the distance across the expanse of green field was Rachel sitting on a blanket. And she wasn't alone.

Johnny squinted to take in the slick-looking professional man in plaid shorts and white polo shirt beside her, *close* beside her.

A burning sensation blistered in Johnny's solar plexus. As the polo-shirted man leaned to look into the picnic basket with Rachel, Johnny felt the powerful impulse to hurl himself across the grass and push the guy away from her.

Just then, Rachel looked in Johnny's direction. Realizing he was in his mechanic's garb, he ducked out of view inside the park building.

Hidden from her, Johnny tried to calm his chaotic breathing. He had no right to get green-eyed over the polo-shirt man with Rachel. No right at all. Not when he was deceiving her about who he really was.

Before he could fume any longer, Mrs. Guillino popped into the building and led him out the back door to her Jag.

For a brief instant, Rachel stared hard in the green-grassed distance. Her heartbeat increased. She could've sworn she'd seen Zane near the park building. But it couldn't have been him. The man she saw was a worker dressed in a stained red shirt and filthy overalls.

She turned back to Chester Zole, the orthopedic surgeon who was her third case study to interview. He was an avid hiker and bicyclist and insisted on holding her interview in the fresh outdoors.

Rachel waved at the yellow jackets buzzing around her lunch. She hated eating outdoors with all those flying and crawling creatures who wanted her food more than she did. Chester was oblivious to the creatures as he bit down on his turkey and lettuce sandwich.

"I never go to bed with a woman unless she showers first," Chester began. "Also, clean fingernails and toenails are a must. And absolutely no perfume in any crevice of her body. My sneezing allergies will not allow it."

Then Chester made a one-hundred-eighty-degree conversation switch to talk about his attending every car show that came to Los Angeles and how he dreamed of owning an electric car someday.

Crawling red ants roamed toward Rachel's lunch on the blanket as she wrote down Chester's responses to her study questions. But her mind drifted to Zane's exotic bathroom where she had surrendered to her need to be physically close to him. She could still feel the torrid heat of his bare-muscled chest against her body. And his tongue erotically dancing inside her mouth. Her mind suddenly drifted into a forbidden fantasy. What would his moist tongue feel like between her thighs?

Stop it! Stop it! she silently scolded herself. No matter how much she wished for a solid forever-relationship with Zane Farrell, the truth thrashed at her heart. A lifetime commitment meant sharing an ongoing fulfilling sex life together. That was a commitment she was incapable of giving any man.

Hurting to the core, Rachel took a huge bite of her tuna salad on a roll—yellow jackets, red ants and all.

* * *

"Jeez!" Johnny cussed loudly as he burnt his finger on
Mr. Farrell's oven. With a pot holder, he grabbed the red-
hot pan and hurled it into the sink, with the metal clanking
against the snow-white porcelain.

Johnny frantically glanced at the kitchen clock. Rachel
would be arriving in a few seconds for another interview.
She'd called him and acted as though nothing had happened between them. He didn't blame her. His behavior had
been inexcusable.

That's why he wanted to surprise her. She was expecting
only an interview. But he'd planned out a whole Zane Farrell dinner. Just to make it up to her.

Mrs. Guillino, his wealthy customer, had saved his rear by
offering her personal recipe for an exquisite dinner. But did
he have her *Bon Appetit* finesse to prepare the courses?

Unfortunately, Johnny was a barbecued hamburger,
Dodger-dog, fried-chicken man. He'd already cindered and
deflated the golden souffléed sole. Now he was attempting
to prepare the *coeur à la creme* with caviar. He laughed out
loud. He couldn't even pronounce the name of the dish
much less cook it.

As he fiddled with the caviar, he couldn't get that polo-
shirt guy out of his mind. Did Rachel have a thing for him?
A burning red heat circulated through his bloodstream. He
couldn't let it matter to him. He didn't stand a chance with
her.

Tonight, he'd force himself to remain detached, the way
Tito had suggested. Once Mr. Farrell returned his call, he'd
get his okay. Then Johnny would reveal his true self to Rachel. That thought bothered him so much that the dish of
black caviar suddenly slipped out of his hands and went
crashing to the floor.

Just then, the door chimes echoed through the mansion,
signaling Rachel's arrival. Johnny rushed to clean up the
mess and put on his best poised Mr. Farrell posture and
opened the door.

But when Johnny set eyes on Rachel, he was a goner. Her chestnut gaze met his like a warm embrace. Her upswept wavy hair shimmered like bronze, and her raspberry lips shone like an inviting dessert. He felt as if not a moment had gone by since he'd last seen her. What ended it was watching her move in that emerald-green knit dress that caressed her curves like a body stocking. Forget the caviar. He wanted *her* for dinner.

"Shall we get right to the sexuality study?" Rachel quickly asked, opening her briefcase, ready to roll.

"Why don't you question me while I'm getting our dinner ready," Johnny suggested.

"You cooked me dinner?" she asked, sounding surprised, her voice softening.

"Sure," he replied, impulsively grabbing her hand and leading her to the patio overlooking the sparkling L.A. evening mountains.

He'd set the table exactly as he'd seen in an exclusive decorating magazine. Radiant candlelight, glittering crystal wineglasses and the finest china.

"Wow," she whispered, her eyes glistening as she turned to him, looking at him like he was someone special, like who he was really mattered to her.

A cool evening breeze blew the strands of Rachel's silken hair across her cheek. Her gardenia perfume permeated the air.

Johnny gently pushed the strands back with his thumb. "You like it?" he asked, his gaze entwined with hers.

"It's—it's perfect," she stammered. Then she kissed him on the lips. The skin on her face turned ashen.

"Rachel," Johnny whispered, gently gliding his thumb along her full bottom lip. But he quickly removed his finger before he did something very un-Mr. Farrell–like. "I hope you don't have other dinner plans tonight." A blistering streak slashed through him again thinking about the polo-shirt guy with her earlier today.

"Not really."

"Are you sure?" he pursued. "Because if you do—"

"I'm positive," she replied. "In fact, I had lunch this afternoon with my third case study."

"How'd it go?" he asked as nonchalantly as he could. If that guy so much as grazed her skin with his pinky, he'd lay him out permanently.

"Actually, it was horrendous," she said, laughing. "I had a red-ant and yellow-jacket sandwich."

Johnny smiled as her bright eyes connected with his almost like they were a couple.

"Then you're starved, I hope," he added.

"Definitely."

"Great!" Johnny said. His dinner idea was going over big. Polo-shirt was just a dull memory in her day. And her eyes were happily sparkling as she looked at him like he was the person she most wanted to be with.

Whoa, he cautioned himself, immediately putting on the emotional brakes. *You've got no holds on her and never will.*

"Wait right here," Johnny instructed as he politely pulled out a patio chair for her.

Back in Mr. Farrell's kitchen, a burning smell hit Johnny's nostrils like an alarm bell. He yanked open the oven door. The gourmet dinner was charred. It figured! Hurriedly, he broiled some steaks he'd bought as backups, fried up onion rings and cooked his specialty, creamed corn and mashed potatoes. It wasn't exactly posh Mr. Farrell style, but heck, it'd taste delicious. And more importantly, Johnny wanted to please Rachel. Not for Mr. Farrell, but for himself. Even if she'd never be his.

From her patio chair, Rachel gazed at the twinkling night lights of L.A. She smiled to herself. She couldn't get over that Zane had cooked dinner for her. He could've easily ordered in expensive cuisine. But he hadn't. He was laboring in the kitchen—all in her honor.

Her heart glowed. What pleased her silly was that his face had relaxed with relief upon hearing that her lunch with case study number three was disastrous. Was Zane truly jealous? Oh, she hoped he was!

Her heartbeat quickened as he entered the patio with both hands overfilled. He was balancing an ice bucket, a bottle of champagne and a corkscrew in one hand, and layers of plates with scrumptious-smelling food in the other.

Suddenly, the plates started to wobble in his hands.

"Let me help," she said. But as she quickly rose from the table, her knee hit the edge of the table, pushing it into Zane, and he was thrown completely off balance.

All at once, the plates of mashed potatoes, fried onion rings and creamed corn went cruising out of his hands straight onto her emerald-green dress.

Splat! Her attire was dripping with yellowish, whitish, wetish gook.

"Oh, no!" Rachel cried. Creamed corn was seeping through the knitted fabric straight through to her bra. Mashed potatoes stuck to her lap with fried onion rings intermixed. She felt all icky and gooey and smelly. She wanted to burst into tears. Her special night with Zane was ruined!

"Don't worry, I'll take care of it!" Johnny immediately said.

He grabbed a dinner napkin and frantically began wiping the creamed corn off the top of her dress.

For a moment, he was so frustrated with himself, so angry for making a mess out of her, that his napkin strokes across her swelling breasts didn't register.

But as he rubbed up and down her chest, he felt her heartbeat pound under his touch. Her nipples protruded from the wet fabric. His manhood suddenly became brazenly alert.

Johnny slowly met her gaze. Her brown eyes were glassy. Her lips parted. Her breath quickened. The napkin slipped from his fingers. He flattened both palms against her hard wet fabric-covered nipples, slowly circling, pressing, until his own breathing became irregular.

She gasped, and closed her eyes for one brief moment as Johnny's wide palms fully enveloped both breasts.

"Rachel," Johnny groaned in her ear. His lips nibbled on her hot earlobe, and his teeth lightly bit the soft skin, wanting to consume her.

Rachel was no longer aware of the sticky mess of her dress. A low moan escaped from her lips as Zane's mouth seared a path down her throat. Tingling sensations rippled through her veins. She was sinking into the sensual reverie of Zane Farrell's touch.

Zane's large palm gently, deliberately, glided down her knit-covered belly. He slowly lifted the hem of her sopping dress. His hand slipped under, and she felt his knuckles graze her bare leg.

She sucked in her breath. She couldn't think. Where was her resistance? Where were her restraints? Her body cried out for him to caress her all over.

Zane's firm hand caressed the flesh of her calf, moving up her leg until he reached the vulnerableness of her inner thigh just inches away from her femininity. Her breaths came short and fast. His probing fingers reached her elastic panty line, about to slip underneath the moist silk.

Suddenly, a loud animalistic cry echoed through the room, and then another, startling her. Her eyes immediately shot open. Her body froze. She realized with utter shock that the uncontrolled sex sounds had come from the depths of her own throat.

Appalled and embarrassed, she eased free of Zane's arms, not wanting to injure his ego this time, not wanting him to think she didn't care, because she did, oh, how she did.

"I—I'm getting chilled in this wet dress," she stammered. "Maybe I'd better go home. I'll come back tomorrow for the interview."

A cloud came over Zane's eyes. She'd hurt him. She hadn't meant to.

"That's not necessary." His voice was husky, still aroused, still wanting her. "There's a washer and dryer near the maid's quarters outside the main house. I'll wash your dress for you. What happened was my fault, anyway."

"No, it was mine," she insisted, not referring to her dress but to her shameful unrelenting lust.

"You're right," he said. "It *was* your fault."

Her body stiffened. Her skin drained with shame. He was referring to her uncontrolled sexual behavior. She wanted to hide from him, from herself.

But then a warm smile deepened the lines of Zane's face as he fingered the sleeve of her dress. And she knew he was kidding around about her clothes, not her sexuality.

"I'll leave out an oversize shirt for you to slip on upstairs," he added.

"Thanks," she replied and then added, "And while I'm waiting for my dress to dry, we'll do the interview."

"See? Our two minds are clicking as one."

In his master bedroom, Zane's words *clicking as one* pleasantly echoed through her head as she removed her icky dress. He'd said it so warmly, so intimately. She liked the idea of being mentally connected to him.

"Hand over your dress," she heard Zane say from the hallway outside the partially closed bedroom door.

She noticed that her silken bra and panties were also stained. She removed her underwear, too. With only the wooden door separating them, she stood defenselessly naked only a few inches from Zane. She extended a bare arm into the hallway to hand him her soiled garments.

He took them, and for a moment, she didn't hear him move outside the bedroom door.

"Ahhh, Rachel," Zane finally said in an awkward tone. "Does your underwear get put in the same wash?"

Rachel held back a giggle. "It's all permanent-press," she replied, enjoying his uncomfortableness with her under-things.

"Right, of course," he said. "I'll meet you in the living room."

As his footsteps bounded down the hall, she immediately called out, "Zane, wait!" But it was too late, the front doors slammed closed. Totally nude, she looked for the shirt he said he'd left for her. It wasn't on the bed. She peeked into his gigantic walk-in closet. The perfectly pressed silk and cotton shirts neatly lined up on hangers looked too ex-pensive to lounge in.

She hurried into the master bathroom to look behind the door for a robe. No robe. Then she stopped and stared at the work shirt and coveralls lying crumpled on the tiled floor. She slowly picked up the oversize red button-down shirt. On the collar, sleeves, chest and back were black grease spots smeared all over.

She felt an odd sensation in her stomach. The shirt re-minded her of something. Yes! The worker she'd seen at Will Rogers State Park. He was wearing the same red shirt and those coveralls!

She shook her head clear. She was being ridiculous. Zane's prestigious business persona would never allow him to be seen in public wearing laborer's unclean attire.

Yet, she couldn't help wondering what an upper-crust man like him was doing with crumpled worker's clothes on his immaculately clean bathroom floor.

With nothing else to wear, she slipped his red shirt over her naked body. Since the shirt was oversize and exceed-ingly long, she didn't need to put on the greasy coveralls. The cotton shirt felt warm against her bare breasts and arms. Her skin oozed heat knowing that only a short time ago that shirt had covered the rippling muscles of Zane's massive chest and back.

* * *

In the laundry room some distance from the main house, Johnny cautiously slipped Rachel's emerald-green dress into the washer. Then he fingered her silken bra. He put his fists inside the cups, feeling the softness and imagining her swelling breasts and taut nipples amply filling each cup. He quickly put her bra into the washer before his fantasies flew out of control.

Then he gingerly picked up her scanty French-cut panties. *Throw them in the water,* he urged himself. The sensual scent of gardenias filled his nostrils.

Cut it out, he scolded himself. *Remember Mr. Farrell's reputation.* He set her panties into the machine with the rest of her soiled clothes and then poured in the laundry detergent.

He certainly hadn't remembered Mr. Farrell's reputation when he was wiping the spilled food from Rachel's dress. The firmness of her abundant breasts and the hot creamy skin of her inner thighs were all Johnny had been thinking about. He couldn't deny it. He desired all of her, every single delectable morsel, because Rachel was everything he could ever imagine in a woman.

He slammed down the washer lid. Maybe as Zane Farrell he could have her, but not as Johnny Wells.

Johnny hurried back to the main house. But when he entered the living room, his legs came to a sudden halt. He gulped when he saw the sight in front of him.

Rachel was sitting comfortably on Mr. Farrell's sofa with her feet tucked under her. Covering her naked body was his red work shirt that he'd absentmindedly thrown on the master-bathroom floor.

Johnny nervously ran his fingers through his curly hair, trying to think fast. How the heck was he going to explain his shop clothes?

"I'll get you a clean shirt," Johnny finally blurted out.

"Oh, no," Rachel insisted. "This one is real comfy." She peered down at the stains. "By the way, how does an elite man like you get dirty spots all over your shirt?"

"My car engine," he shot out, searching for a viable story and hating himself for it. "When I fiddled with some faulty parts, grease splashed on my shirt." It was *partly* true.

"Really? You work on your car sometimes?" she said. "Were you by any chance at Will Rogers State Park this afternoon?"

Johnny's insides tensed like a strained rubber band. "The park?"

"I saw a man wearing the same stained red shirt and those coveralls that are up in your bathroom," she explained. "It's nuts, I know, but I thought he was you."

Johnny wanted to yell out that it *was* him. That he wasn't Zane Farrell. That he was just a worker who made his mediocre living with his hard-callused hands. But his promise to Mr. Farrell kept him handcuffed.

"I thought dirty red shirts were *in* these days?" he jokingly responded, almost choking on his chuckle.

"I guess they are," she replied, smiling. "But sometimes I wonder about you, Zane."

"Really? About what?" Johnny asked. *Man, oh, man, here it comes.*

"Somehow, you don't fit with this outrageously wealthy environment."

"Are you hurling a sideways insult at me?"

"No, no," she quickly said. "It's just an observation."

"Where *do* you picture me?" The band in his stomach was about to snap.

"I don't know," she pondered out loud. "Maybe in a cozy cabin in the woods."

"With you?" he said kiddingly. He wanted to take her mind off the obvious, but then he realized he meant what he'd said. More than anything, he wanted to spend more than one day with her, like a week, a month, a year.

She remained silent, avoiding his eyes, nervously fidgeting with her notepad and pen. He'd made her feel uncomfortable, exactly what he didn't want to do.

"Hey, how about your sex questions?" Johnny asked, sitting down cross-legged on the floor across from her, craving to forget his red shirt, the grease stains and the despicable lies.

Rachel grabbed her briefcase and set it on the sofa beside her. She hadn't responded to him because staying overnight in a cozy cabin with him was exactly what she had in mind, too. But the idea scared her. And sex was the reason.

Her palms were sweaty as she anxiously glanced at her question pad. She wanted to steer their minds away from sex, but there was no way with the next study question staring her in the face.

"What excites you most about a woman?" she managed to say.

Zane rubbed his hands on his knees. "Do you mean which body part?"

"Well, yes," she replied a bit unsteadily.

"Your—I mean, a woman's breasts," Zane replied, looking straight at her.

She swallowed as his gaze drifted from her eyes to the front of his red shirt. In her haste, she'd left the top three buttons open and a hint of bare cleavage peeked out at him.

Her stomach quivered. Was he fantasizing about caressing her breasts that very second? She quickly scanned question number two. Couldn't she skip that one? But the study demanded further details.

"Exactly what turns you on about that particular female body part?"

"When I touch a woman's breasts?"

"Yes," she croaked, scribbling notes she could barely see on the page.

As she shifted uncomfortably on the sofa, the fabric of his cotton shirt rubbed against her nipples almost like the feel of his hands. Her face heated up. She could barely breathe.

"Actually, what excites me most is when I cover her naked breasts with my bare—" Zane stopped talking. A frown crossed his forehead. "Rachel, do you really want to hear this stuff? If it makes you feel uneasy—"

"I'm fine, really," she insisted. "I need these details for the study." But she was dying inside, yearning to hear more. Yet, his every word was making it harder and harder not to think about making love to him.

"I get really turned on when a woman's nipples grow stiff and hard against my bare palms." He held out his strong wide hands as though wanting to caress her breasts to demonstrate.

A hot tingle fluttered through her. She could barely read the next question.

"Why—why is that so arousing to you?"

"Because of her."

"What about her?"

"What arouses me the most," he said, staring into her eyes, "is exciting a woman to such intensity that she's crying out with orgasm after orgasm. I want her to be completely satisfied when our lovemaking is over."

Rachel's pen stopped moving on the pad. She couldn't remember what she'd written down. Her skin was steaming with the need to be in his arms, holding him, caressing him.

"Zane, it's getting late," she said, unable to continue hearing another erotic word. "I'm a bit tired." Tired? She was ready to tear off his clothes!

"Sure, of course," Johnny said. He was about to rise but suddenly sat back down. He didn't dare get up from that floor. His sex talk with her had aroused him to the point where his male part was straining against his jeans ready to burst.

He waited a few moments to calm down his body. But Rachel started to get up from the sofa, and the red shirt covering her naked body momentarily slipped up her legs.

Johnny sucked in his breath as her tender chestnut patch peeked out at him. His maleness pulsated against his zipper with the urgent need to be deep, deep inside her.

Johnny jumped up from the floor and rushed for the double copper doors. "I'll check on your clothes!"

The moment Johnny was outside in the fresh night air, he leaned against the trunk of a sky-high palm tree. Breathing heavily, he tried to regain his composure. How could he sit that close to her luscious body all naked and vulnerable under his red shirt and not desire her? He'd never wanted to be close to a woman so much in his entire life.

Johnny walked briskly to the maid's quarters. He checked to make sure that Rachel's emerald-green dress was ready for the dryer. He lifted out her wet sheer panties and damp lacy bra with his hot fingers. He ached with torment for the body that filled those garments.

Back at the house, Rachel was so aroused, she couldn't deal with the sex questionnaire anymore. As she stuffed her pad and pen into her briefcase, the pleasure area between her thighs throbbed for Zane's masculinity.

If he'd tried to make love to her, would she have had the inner strength to resist him? She knew she wouldn't. But he hadn't tried. Why?

Because Zane Farrell respected her as the professor of the study, that's why. She'd never met a man so honorable. And she trusted him implicitly. He was the very type of man she dreamed of sharing the rest of her days with.

What was she thinking? Zane had told her that he needed to completely satisfy a woman in bed. That woman could never be her. Not when her erogenous desires had already destroyed one relationship.

Rachel's thoughts were abruptly interrupted by the ringing of Zane's silver portable telephone. She quickly turned to the copper doors. Zane still wasn't back from the laundry room. The phone kept ringing. She rushed to the front window searching for him. The night was dark. The palm trees were still. Only shadowy lamplight flickered on the empty pathway leading to the maid's quarters.

The ringing wouldn't stop. Should she answer it for him?

Finally, thinking he wouldn't mind, she gingerly lifted the silver receiver and put it to her ear.

From the laundry room, Johnny heard the ringing of Mr. Farrell's telephone echo across the estate. He grabbed the phone in the maid's room but slammed it down when he heard a dial tone and realized the maid had a separate number.

Johnny frantically dashed outside toward the main house. The ringing had stopped. The night was stagnantly silent. He could barely smell the candied rosebushes in the air. Sweat beads formed on his forehead. His heart was pumping. Had Rachel dared to answer the phone? He prayed like a demon that she hadn't. He couldn't let her find out the truth about him through a damn phone call!

Johnny yanked open the front doors almost off their hinges. As he raced inside the house, he suddenly realized that Rachel's moist silk panties and bra were still between his fingertips.

Four

Johnny's heart pounded against his rib cage as he dashed into the living room.

"You want to speak to who?" Rachel asked, pressing the silver portable closer to her ear. "We've got a terrible connection. Can you speak a little louder?"

When she saw Johnny, she put her hand over the receiver and said, "It's someone calling from Cairo."

Johnny went brain-dead. Before he could retrieve the phone from her, she immediately put her lips to the receiver again. "Who did you say you want to talk to? Johnny? Johnny Wells? There's nobody—"

"I'll take it," Johnny managed to say as he recovered the phone from her. "Can I help you?" he said into the phone, giving Rachel a shrug, as if he had no idea who was on the other end. Then he casually walked over to the sliding glass door as though gazing out at the pool.

The static on the portable with the weak battery made it difficult for Johnny to hear Mr. Farrell's voice from Cairo.

"Please forgive me for interrupting your evening, Johnny," Mr. Farrell said. "I received your message. Is there a matter that demands my immediate attention?"

"I need to speak with you, but—" Johnny glanced at Rachel who was sitting on the sofa flipping through an architectural magazine.

"Obviously, I have called at an off-color moment," Mr. Farrell interjected. "I am terribly sorry. I shall phone when you are less involved."

"That'd be great," Johnny said, keeping his back to Rachel. "When can you call back?"

"I will—" Suddenly, the static on the phone blipped out. And so did Mr. Farrell.

"Hello?" Johnny whispered into the phone. "Hello?" He banged on the phone. His stomach twisted into a tight knot. The phone battery was dead!

Man, oh, man! Johnny silently screamed. He was so frustrated, he wanted to hurl the phone into the kidney-shaped pool.

"What's wrong?" Rachel asked in a concerned voice.

"Not a thing," Johnny quickly replied, trying not to let on that his intestines were ready to explode.

"Who's Johnny?" she innocently inquired.

"Huh?" His hand squeezed the silver portable until his knuckles turned bloodred.

"Johnny Wells," she added. "The person the man on the phone was asking for."

"Oh, *him,*" Johnny said, desperately searching for an answer to give her.

His mind thundered with revulsion at the thought of lying to her again. But he hadn't gotten the chance to clear the truth with Mr. Farrell yet. That's what killed him. He'd had Mr. Farrell right at his ear, and he couldn't resolve the pressing problem!

"Does Johnny Wells live in this house, too?" she asked. "You never told me—"

"No, no," Johnny cut in. "He's, well, he's the full-time chauffeur. But he's on vacation. I guess the guy on the phone was a family member or something."

Johnny avoided her believing eyes. He was disgusted at himself for being dishonest. He set the dead phone on the end table wondering how the hell he was going to get out of this mess.

Suddenly, Rachel burst into laughter, ripping into him like sharp shearing scissors. Had he blown it? Had she seen right through his implausible story?

She clasped her mouth with her hand trying to hold back her hysterics.

"What's so funny?" he asked abruptly.

"It's you!" she said, bursting into convulsive laughter again.

"What about me?" he asked, dreading her next words. Did he look like that much of a fool in her eyes?

Giggling like crazy, she pointed a shaky finger at him. "Look—look at your hand!" she squealed.

Annoyed with her jeering and mocking, he angrily glanced at his hand in confusion.

Hot blood rushed to Johnny's face as he stared at his left hand. His fist was stuffed inside the cup of her moist silk bra, from his laundry-room antics imagining the ample size of her breasts. And her wet French-cut panties were dangling from his wrist.

Johnny's cerebellum turned to watery oatmeal. An excuse came rushing out in a surge of sheer guilt.

"I was putting the phone in the dryer when I heard your underwear ringing," he clumsily explained.

"Oh, really," she said with a giggle.

Realizing he'd fumbled it but good, he said sheepishly, "Okay, okay, you caught me with your underwear. Just more material for your sex study, right?"

"Do you *always* play with a woman's bra and panties?" she teasingly asked with a sensual twinkle in her eyes.

"Only underwear with the scent of gardenia," Johnny replied, his gaze boldly steady on her.

Rachel's heart flip-flopped at Zane's direct reference to her perfume. Seeing his strong masculine fingers clutching her bra and panties made her thighs automatically squeeze together in pleasure. Her skin burned under the red shirt as she wondered what erotic thoughts he'd harbored while fondling her moist undergarments.

Zane nervously cleared his throat as he gathered her underwear in both hands. "I'll get your clothes dried in record time," he told her, then hurried out of the house.

Rachel pulled the red shirt tightly around her body. Something felt strange to her. Gingerly, she fingered the silver phone. Ever since that call, she sensed an oddness in Zane's behavior. When she'd inquired about the Cairo caller and who Johnny Wells was, Zane had seemed nervous. She couldn't shake the feeling that he was trying to hide something from her.

Rachel quickly took her hand off the phone and silently scolded herself. Zane's business was his own, wasn't it? She had no claims on him. Yet, she yearned to know more about his private life. He never talked to her about what went on when she wasn't around.

She slid both hands down the front of his soiled red shirt, wondering about the man who lived inside that shirt. Zane Farrell was a mystery. Why hadn't he revealed more about himself to her?

Zane returned to the house with her dried dress and underwear. She wanted to talk further, but he seemed preoccupied, as if he was anxious for her to leave. He obviously didn't feel close enough to her to share more of his life with her. But what right did she have to complain? There was a part of her she'd never reveal to anyone—especially Zane Farrell.

* * *

When Rachel returned to her university office, Kim took Zane's file from her to review Rachel's day's work.

"Rachel," Kim hesitantly began as she gazed at the papers Rachel had written on Zane. "I get the strong feeling that you want to make love to Zane Farrell."

"What—what did you say?" Rachel stammered, stunned by her friend's words.

"Look at this," Kim said, picking up one of the papers on Zane Farrell that Rachel had filled out. "In answer to your question to Farrell, 'What turns you on most about a woman?' you wrote that Zane Farrell's response was, 'The growing bulge in his pants is making me so hot I'm going to have an orgasm!'"

"Let me see that!" Rachel said, grabbing the paper and staring at her notes in utter shock.

Instead of recording Zane's sexual interest in a woman's breasts, she'd unconsciously written down *her* sensual response to his answer.

With a blazing face of embarrassment, Rachel crumpled up the paper and hurled it into the trash can.

"Rachel, what are you doing?" Kim asked in horror as she pulled out the paper from the trash.

"I'll write it over," she said. "I can remember his answers." She slumped down in her chair, feeling devastated by her blatant admission on paper.

"Your scribbles are no big deal, Rachel," Kim said with concern.

"What if you hadn't caught it, Kim?" she frantically asked. "What if the chancellor had seen my X-rated comment? I'd be fired off the project and maybe off the campus, too!"

What was happening to her? Was she so blurred by sexual arousal that she couldn't even control what she wrote down?

"Forget it, will you?" Kim insisted.

"I can't."

"Why?" her friend asked. "Was his bulge *that* big?" Kim tried to look serious, but she broke out into a mischievous grin.

"*Very* big," Rachel couldn't help replying with an equally devilish smile.

They both erupted into giggles. But behind her laughter, Rachel was worried. There was no doubt that she yearned to make love to Zane Farrell, but she also knew that she could never fulfill that dream. Because if she ever tried, she'd lose Zane forever.

Johnny entered the electric-car show at the Los Angeles Convention Center with Mrs. Guillino. He tried to concentrate on her conversation as thousands of chattering and laughing visitors surrounded them.

"Johnny, do you think my husband would be interested in that electric car?" Mrs. Guillino asked, pointing to a yellow electric car.

"Let me see," Johnny replied as he checked out the spec sheet on the vehicle.

The Guillinos were considering purchasing an electric car but needed Johnny's automotive expertise. Mrs. Guillino's husband had asked Johnny to accompany her to the car show since he was too swamped with work to go himself.

Mr. Guillino had insisted on paying for Johnny's convention time, but Johnny had emphatically refused the lucrative offer. The Guillinos' steady business at his shop was payment enough. Doing them a favor was his pleasure.

"Look at the sleek body on that car!" Mrs. Guillino exclaimed, pointing to the glossy red job on display.

Johnny's mind shifted to something else very sleek. A mental image of Rachel's naked body underneath his red work shirt flashed through his head. He imagined her lush bare buttocks just inches from his grasp. Her satiny, firm thighs. The pink flesh peeking out at him from between her legs.

And those sparkling brown eyes pulling him in without a hint of resistance.

"Johnny, are you listening?" Mrs. Guillino asked, cutting into his sexual fantasies.

"Absolutely, Mrs. Guillino," he quickly replied.

But he barely heard her next words. He was worried about Mr. Farrell's last call at the Bel Air mansion. What if Rachel had found out the truth about him through one stupid phone call?

Johnny had forced Rachel into leaving Mr. Farrell's house sooner than he'd really wanted because he was afraid Mr. Farrell would call again while she was there. He'd waited all night at the mansion for Mr. Farrell to call back, but he never did.

Now Johnny had to continue his polluted lies to Rachel.

"Johnny, how do these electric cars operate?" Mrs. Guillino asked, abruptly tearing into his tortured thoughts.

"The first major advantage, of course, is that an electric car doesn't need gasoline," Johnny began. Then he expounded on the various advantages and disadvantages of electric cars.

Johnny had Mrs. Guillino's rapt attention. She was an attractive woman a few years older than him. She had fluffy blond hair, green eyes, and she sparkled with dazzling diamond stud earrings, choker necklace and diamond bracelet.

Johnny felt comfortable being at the show with Mrs. Guillino because she was very much in love with her husband and viewed Johnny purely as her mechanic. In fact, when one of the exhibitors referred to Johnny as Mrs. Guillino's husband, she quickly corrected the exhibitor about Johnny's role as her car mechanic.

Johnny didn't blame her for setting the guy straight. Even though he was wearing his best duds, Johnny still felt like a worker. He was definitely not a member of Mrs. Guillino's upper-echelon society. And what injured him the most was knowing that he could never belong to Rachel's world of academia.

The parking lot of the convention center was jammed with cars sizzling under the L.A. sun. Dr. Chester Zole found a parking spot and held open the door of his midnight-black sports Jeep for Rachel to climb out.

Rachel had visited Chester at his condo for another interview, but Chester had insisted she continue her questioning at a car show he didn't want to miss.

As Rachel followed Chester into the massive L.A. Convention Center, her attention was riveted on the glittering electric cars on display. Chester talked on and on about his interest in high-tech automobiles and how his expensive cars always made a sensual impression on the women he dated.

Chester held Rachel's arm to guide her across the jammed convention floor. Suddenly, through the maze of visitor faces, Zane Farrell's face loomed out at her.

Her heart raced. Her cheeks warmed at the sight of him. She was about to rush over to him, when she noticed that he wasn't alone. Beside him was a high-society blonde whispering in his ear.

Rachel stopped walking. She was no longer aware of the thousands of convention visitors. All she saw was Zane animatedly talking to the attractive blonde as if he knew her well—very well.

The blonde radiated a soft sensuality as she gently touched Zane's arm while she spoke. Zane appeared content in her presence—like a sexually satisfied male.

Rachel's blood curdled. She could barely feel Chester's hand on her arm. Even though she knew she had no hold on Zane, somehow, she still felt betrayed. Hadn't he led her to believe that he was not involved with anyone? Hadn't he passionately kissed her and caressed her burning skin? Hadn't he even fondled her underwear?

Her mind was suddenly blinded by emotion. She streaked her way through the crowd with a confused Chester still holding on to her arm.

Johnny was walking with Mrs. Guillino to the next car exhibit, when a woman barreling through the crowd suddenly caught the corner of his eye. He did a major double take. He couldn't believe his eyes!

Rachel was heading straight for him with her polo-shirt case study tagging along.

What the hell do I do? echoed through his brain. How could he introduce Mrs. Guillino to Rachel? What if Mrs. Guillino called him Johnny in front of her?

Johnny's thoughts exploded into confused fragments inside his head. Mrs. Guillino was asking him about one of the cars, but he had to think fast about Rachel.

Just then, Rachel was pulled back by polo-shirt. He directed her attention to a car exhibit that had caught his interest.

Johnny quickly turned to Mrs. Guillino. "Would you excuse me for just a—"

"Johnny," Mrs. Guillino interrupted. "I see an acquaintance of mine. I shall return in a sec." Then she disappeared in the crowd.

He was just about to search for Rachel when he heard her voice behind him.

"Zane, I didn't know you were a car enthusiast."

He whirled, ready to explain, but his words never had a chance to exit his mouth. Just being near her again made his soul beam. Her intoxicating gardenia perfume sent him flying to the point where he forgot about Mrs. Guillino.

"Rachel, it's great to see you," Johnny said.

"Where's your *date?*" she inquired.

"My what?" Johnny asked.

Johnny couldn't believe it. Rachel was getting green-eyed over Mrs. Guillino. A glint of pleasure shot through him.

"The cute blonde," she went on, trying to act cool, but Johnny could see she was steaming.

"Rachel, are you jealous?" Johnny couldn't resist asking.

"What?" she said. "Absolutely not!"

"Not even just a little?" he teased.

"I'm interested only because of the university study," she quickly told him.

"Sure. Uh-huh. For the study."

"That's right," she insisted, her brown eyes burning with fury.

"You're beautiful when you're jealous, you know that?" Johnny said, wanting to crush her soft body to his right there and then.

"Then I can write in my research paper that you *are* seeing the blonde," she continued, her voice shaking a little.

Suddenly, Johnny remembered Mrs. Guillino and glanced around the room to locate her. When he spotted her, his nervous system totally malfunctioned.

Mrs. Guillino was talking to Rachel's polo-shirt case study as though they were old buddies!

Johnny quickly grabbed Rachel's arm. "Hey, would you look at this electric car?" he said, trying to lead her into the shield of the thick crowd.

Rachel immediately pulled free of his hand.

"What are you running away from?" she asked.

"Nothing," Johnny replied, hating those lies again.

"Don't you want to introduce me to your date?" she asked. She turned her attention in the direction Johnny dreaded for her to look in.

"I can't believe it," Rachel said, surprised. "Your date knows Chester."

Johnny grabbed her by the shoulders and made her face him.

"Rachel, she's not my date," he told her. "She's not my woman. She's just a friend."

"Really?" she hesitantly asked, her voice softening. "You and her are not—" She nervously blinked a few times and suddenly looked so vulnerable that he wanted to hold her.

At that moment, Johnny knew Rachel was beginning to care for him. His heart burst into a melodic song.

"No, Rachel, she and I are not—"

Just then, a visitor sifting through the crowded room knocked into Rachel, pushing her into Johnny. Her firm breasts crushed against his chest. Her soft hands clutched his taut arms. Her rosebud lips were inches from his mouth.

Johnny forgot he was Mr. Farrell. He forgot he was with Mrs. Guillino. He pulled Rachel tightly to him and grazed her mouth with his. Her lips welcomely parted for his kiss. And he hungrily tasted the sweet, sweet gardenia of her.

"Ah-hem!" a male voice broke into their reverie.

Johnny immediately released Rachel. The polo-shirt guy was standing there looking a bit awkward.

"Oh, Chester," Rachel said, rubbing her red lipstick smudge from Johnny's lips. "I'd like you to meet my other case study, Zane Farrell."

"Pleasure," Chester said to Johnny, extending his surgeon's hand and looking questioningly at the two of them.

"Good meeting you, Chester," Johnny told him.

As Johnny shook Chester's hand, he anxiously looked around the room for Mrs. Guillino. She was standing only a few feet away from them checking out a yellow electric car as an eager salesperson made her pitch.

Johnny's ribs tightened under his shirt.

"I've got to get going," he hurriedly said to Rachel. "I'll call to confirm your next interview."

Before Rachel could respond, Zane ran off into the crowd. She unconsciously touched her lips where he'd just kissed her. A warmth enveloped her. Their brief exchange wasn't just physical to her. She felt a closeness with Zane, a closeness she'd never felt before.

As she followed Chester out of the convention center to his Jeep in the parking lot, she realized that she hadn't found out who Zane's blond friend was.

"Chester, who was the woman you were talking to?" she curiously asked.

"Adrienne Guillino," Chester replied as he unlocked the Jeep door for her. "She and her husband used to be patients of mine."

"She's married?" she asked in a surprised tone as she climbed into the Jeep. She wondered why Zane hadn't told her.

"Adrienne's been wedded for twenty long, long years," Chester replied. Then he laughed and added, "No wonder she was with a younger guy."

"What do you mean?" Rachel asked, suddenly feeling uneasy.

"I don't know why Adrienne didn't go to the car show with her husband," Chester remarked as he drove the Jeep out of the parking lot. "He's an avid car fan, like me."

"Zane said she was a friend."

"That's not what she told me." He glanced at her in a very suspicious manner.

Rachel tensed up in the seat. "Who did she say Zane was to her?"

Johnny could finally breathe normally. Rachel and polo-shirt had left the convention center. His heart returned to a steady rhythm. That was too close a call for him. He had to be more careful with his Mr. Farrell role, not only to protect Mr. Farrell, but Johnny never wanted to hurt Rachel, not ever.

He led Mrs. Guillino over to the food-concession area and bought them each a cup of coffee.

"Chester Zole is such a marvelous physician," Mrs. Guillino commented. "What a coincidence that you know the professor he was with."

"Isn't it?" Johnny preferred to stay off that topic but good. "Can I get you a cupcake or something?" he asked, then took a sip of his coffee.

"I think dear Chester had the wrong idea about us," Mrs. Guillino added in an amused tone.

Johnny stared at her. "What do you mean?"

"I got the distinct impression that Chester thought you were my secret lover."

"Really?" Johnny said, nervously downing the rest of his coffee in one swallow.

"Don't worry, I made the reality of the situation perfectly clear to dear Charlie," she explained.

Johnny's lungs stopped functioning. "What exactly did you tell him?"

"That you are my car mechanic, of course."

Johnny crushed the foam cup in his hand until it crackled into tiny snowflake fragments.

Five

"**M**rs. Guillino said that Zane was her *car mechanic*?" Rachel repeated to Chester. "I—I don't understand."

The Jeep went over a bump in the road, bouncing Rachel's confused thoughts into further disarray.

"I think Adrienne is having an affair with him," Chester began. "She's afraid if I find out, it will get back to her husband."

Just then, Chester's car phone rang, and he picked it up.

Rachel turned away from Chester and stared out the Jeep's window. But all she saw was one big L.A. blur. Doubts about Zane ricocheted back and forth in her skull.

Zane said Mrs. Guillino was just a friend. Yet, why didn't he tell her that Mrs. Guillino was married? And why would Mrs. Guillino label him as her car mechanic?

Rachel nervously bit her bottom lip. She wanted to believe that Zane was honest with her. Their kiss on the convention floor had felt so real, so intimate. So why couldn't she shake the nagging feeling that he was hiding something from her?

At the car shop, Johnny's elderly customer thanked him profusely for repairing her faulty vehicle. But when the customer tried to start up her car to leave his shop, her engine was stone-dead.

When Johnny lifted the hood of her car, his face burned with embarrassment. He'd forgotten to put back her car battery.

Tito peered at him sideways. Johnny rarely made mistakes at the shop. He took pride in that fact. But not now. Not when he was worried blind that Rachel might know the truth of his real identity.

He didn't want her finding out from someone else. He had to be the one to tell her.

That night at his Santa Monica apartment, Johnny called Rachel's office at the university. He knew she wouldn't be there. But he needed to hear her voice, even if it was only a recording.

When the machine beeped for his message, he hesitated a moment. "Rachel, I'll pick you up at the Sunset Boulevard exit of the university for our next interview, like we planned. See you then."

Johnny slowly hung up, hating himself for continuing the lies. Yet, he was forced to act as if he was still Zane Farrell until Mr. Farrell gave him the okay to do otherwise.

He slammed out of his apartment. He walked for blocks and blocks in the evening darkness trying to ignore the bolt of pain coursing through his body at the thought that maybe Rachel already knew who he really was.

In the morning, Rachel listened carefully to Zane's message on her office answering machine. She rewound it and played it over and over again. Did Zane sound like a liar? No, he didn't. He couldn't. But there was hesitation in his voice, almost sadness, and she desperately wanted to understand why.

She replayed his message one more time, and then another, and another, wishing she could see his face. Maybe then she'd know what was going on.

"Rachel, what are you doing?" Kim said, standing at the door watching her.

The skin on her face got hot. "I—I can't understand Zane's message. I was just playing it over to—"

"Rachel, this is Kim you're talking to."

She clicked off the machine. "I thought I knew him, Kim. But I'm not sure anymore."

"What happened?"

"I don't know if he's being sincere with me." She plopped down on her desk chair, feeling hopeless. She explained about the car show, Mrs. Guillino, how Zane had said that Mrs. Guillino was only a friend, and then Mrs. Guillino's calling him her car mechanic.

"Maybe you're misinterpreting the entire situation," Kim told her.

"It's more than that, Kim," Rachel went on. "I feel like he's deliberately keeping parts of his life from me. And I don't know why."

"You know what I think?" Kim asked, sitting on Rachel's desk top. "I think you're falling in love with him."

Rachel's heart pounded at hearing the truth of her friend's words. "Kim, what am I going to do?"

"Give him a chance to explain his side," her friend suggested. "That's what I do when I'm feeling unsure or doubt Charlie. Once I hear him out, I'm fine."

"Oh, Kim," she said, standing up and hugging her. "I hope you're right."

But she was worried about the research project, too. With all her concerns about Zane, she wasn't concentrating on the sex study as she should. But it was so hard to when all she wanted to do was think about her and Zane.

* * *

The Pacific Ocean sparkled like diamonds as Johnny drove Rachel along the coastline in Mr. Farrell's red Porsche. She'd been staring out the window ever since he'd picked her up.

A nightmare of darkness filled Johnny's skull. What was she thinking? Did she know the dirty truth about him? If she didn't, wouldn't she be looking him straight in the face?

Though the white sand and blue ocean were a stunning picturesque view, to Johnny, the most beautiful sight of all was Rachel sitting next to him.

The ocean wind blew back her wavy chestnut hair. For the first time, her hair was unrestrained by a bun. She'd let her shiny tresses flow like silk onto her shoulders. Her elegant hands nervously clutched her briefcase on her lap.

Johnny squeezed the steering wheel so tight his fingers screamed in pain. He wanted to reach out and caress her softness. He wanted to tell her that he wasn't a liar. That he was just doing his job.

Johnny drove the car off the Pacific Coast Highway high up a hill toward the L.A. Art Museum. He remembered Mr. Farrell's chauffeur, George, once telling him that Mr. Farrell often visited the museum. At times, Mr. Farrell had even loaned out pieces of famous artwork for viewing at the museum.

Since Johnny had no other choice but to continue being Mr. Farrell, he decided to play the role to the fullest. He was taking her to the museum for her interview.

Johnny had made a quick run to the library before picking up Rachel. He'd sifted through art books to familiarize himself with van Gogh, Rodin, and Rembrandt so he could at least exhibit a trace of Mr. Farrell's cultured persona.

The colossal museum appeared in front of him like an exquisite Roman villa. Eucalyptus and pine trees cushioned the European-style structure like nature's pillows.

Johnny walked next to Rachel up the wooded path toward the museum, not knowing how to break the tense silence. Rachel suddenly stopped and faced him.

"Zane, will you be honest with me?" she asked. He could hear her voice trembling a little, and he blamed himself.

"Of course," Johnny replied, swallowing hard. *Tell her straight out that you didn't mean to fool her,* he silently urged himself. *She's hurting, and it's all because of you.*

"I need to know the truth," she went on.

Johnny was just about to ask, What truth? but he knew. Yet, he still had to keep up the fakery. He hated it! He wanted to be *real* with her.

Instead, honoring to his obligation to Mr. Farrell, he asked, "Is this about your sex test?"

"No." She looked up at him with troubled eyes. "Mrs. Guillino told Chester that you're her car mechanic."

"Really?" he said, despising his fraudulent reaction, but knowing he had no other choice.

"Why would she call a man of your prestige a car repairman?"

Johnny nervously ran his fingers through his curly hair. "She must have been joking around." He could still see doubt in her eyes.

"Why would she? For what reason?"

The grinding in Johnny's stomach increased. He knew he should chuck his commitment to Mr. Farrell and tell her right then and there that he was Johnny Wells. But he couldn't break his word.

"Sometimes I help repair Mrs. Guillino's car."

"You do?" she asked. Then she thought for a moment, and her eyes lit up. "Yes—your red work shirt. You said you tinkered with engines."

"Of course," Johnny said. "Come on. Do I look like a car mechanic?"

Johnny waited with tense muscles. Part of him wanted her to say yes because then she'd be seeing the real him. But the other part wished she'd see a cultured, poised man like Mr. Farrell—the kind of man he could see her being with.

Rachel hesitated answering. There was something about Zane that made him so un-entrepreneurish. Was it the raw ruggedness of him? Was it the way his curly hair was always just a little mussed? She couldn't pinpoint it.

"What is it, Rachel?" Zane asked.

"I feel like there's so much I don't know about you," she heard herself say.

"What else do you want to know?" he quickly asked. "That I think about you all the time?"

Her heart missed a beat. "Do you?"

Zane nodded. "Being with you is what I look forward to the most."

Johnny knew it definitely wasn't what Mr. Farrell would've said, but that's how Johnny felt at that moment. And damned if he was going to hide that truth about himself!

Then, on the wooded path to the L.A. Art Museum, surrounded by tall eucalyptus trees, Johnny drew Rachel into his arms and covered her mouth with his. He needed to feel her close. He needed to know she was still there for him.

Rachel's lips parted for Zane's kiss. She tasted the mintiness of him. The warmth of his arms around her and the revelation of his words sent a solid message to her. Zane was beginning to care for her as much as she was for him.

Zane nibbled at her earlobe, sending shivers up her spine. She sucked in her breath as he undid the top two buttons of her pink blouse. He slid his moist lips to the crevice of her breasts. He licked the swollen flesh above her lacy bra.

Rachel circled his neck with her arms and edged his face closer to her throbbing breasts.

"Zane," she whispered, wanting to tell him how close she felt to him.

Suddenly, there were footsteps and museum visitors' voices nearby. Rachel quickly broke apart from Zane. He struggled to button her pink blouse before the people appeared.

Just then, an elderly man and woman walking arm-in-arm approached them on the path. One of Rachel's pink buttons snapped off her blouse and flew out of Zane's hand. The button landed on the ground right at the shoes of the elderly couple.

Zane sheepishly smiled at them, picked up the button and hurriedly handed it to Rachel. She fumbled putting it into her briefcase.

The elderly couple, still hand-in-hand, smiled knowingly at each other and walked past.

Rachel giggled. "They must have thought we were naughty," she said.

"We were."

Zane pulled her up against him and gave her a soft kiss on the mouth, as though he didn't care who saw them embracing. Then he took her hand and squeezed it—as if they were a couple—a younger version of the elderly one.

As she strolled with Zane through the museum's fountain garden, he clutched her waist and tugged her closer to his body. She leaned her head comfortably against his shoulder. Her hand rested on his hip.

At that moment, she forgot all about the sex study. She was only aware of Zane next to her, and the blossoming emotional link she shared with him.

Just as they reached the magnificent paintings and sculptures inside the museum, she suddenly felt Zane tense beside her. He gently released her body and glanced at his watch.

"Can we do your interview another day?" he asked. "I forgot about a business matter I need to take care of."

"S-sure," she replied in a disappointed voice.

When he dropped her off at the campus, his kiss was cool, leaving her confused about his sudden withdrawal.

* * *

Johnny raced off the university grounds in Mr. Farrell's Porsche. He knew Rachel felt let down by his abrupt departure. It killed him to leave her like that. But he had to do it.

He was feeling so close to her that he would've taken her back to Mr. Farrell's mansion and made incredible love to her. There was no doubt in his mind about that. But he knew the peril of fulfilling his deepest desire. She would think she was making love to Zane Farrell—not to Johnny Wells. And that would hurt more than he could tolerate.

In the university lecture hall, Rachel asked her students, "Can anyone tell me the sociological cause of the deterioration of the gangs in our country?" She looked at all of their thoughtful faces. "At one time, gangs were groups of friends who shared the same interests and hung out together. Now a gang is associated with fear and violence. Any ideas on the reasons for this change?"

Rachel leaned on the podium as two students began the discussion. No matter how hard she tried, she couldn't focus on the voices in her class.

Zane popped into her mind. She wondered why he'd cut their time together so short at the L.A. Art Museum. Had he sensed a more-than-overwhelming need in her kisses? Was she already scaring him away?

A cramp lightninged through her stomach. She couldn't let her excessive sexual nature ruin it between them. But how could she control her desires when she wanted him so very much?

Rachel forced her attention back to the two students verbally sparring about the gang issue. As she struggled to listen to their debate, she tried to forget Zane for just a little while.

Kim was anxiously waiting for her the moment Rachel came out of the building. She pulled Rachel to the side, away from the rushing students and professors.

"Rachel, you're not going to want to hear this."

"What is it?"

"The state cut the university's budget," Kim said in a rush. "The research money for the sex study was the first to go."

"Wh-what does that mean to my research?" she stammered, her stomach tightening, not only for the love of her project, but because of how it would affect her relationship with Zane.

"You've been given only one more interview with each of your three case studies."

"Oh, no," she whispered. "Not now." Not when she and Zane were just beginning to discover each other.

Thick black liquid from the bottom of a customer's car poured into the metal pan as Johnny stood under the hydraulic lift. Grease spots were all over his face and hands as he changed the oil.

He hurriedly yanked out the oil pan from beneath the car. He had called Cairo that morning. A real estate agent had phoned Mr. Farrell about an important property. But Johnny was too late. Mr. Farrell had signed out of the Cairo hotel for Paris.

Now Johnny was forced to meet with the real estate lady on Mr. Farrell's behalf. She said that a prime real-estate-property deal would fall through if Mr. Farrell didn't make an immediate decision.

In a flurry of energy, Johnny left the shop to Tito, went to Mr. Farrell's Bel Air house and flipped through the business files Mr. Farrell had given him permission to peruse when necessary. He sat down on the plush silver carpeting in Mr. Farrell's office and carefully studied every tidbit of information he could find.

Within minutes, Johnny got an overview on Mr. Farrell's real estate property the agent was referring to. He dashed into the shower and then hoisted on a suit and tie. He hoped to hell that he could pull this one off.

By the time the real estate broker arrived to pick him up, Johnny was all decked out Mr. Farrell–style, ready to go.

Standing in front of the commercial office building in West Los Angeles that Mr. Farrell owned, Johnny was stunned when the broker suggested he sell the ten-million-dollar building. The buyer was offering fifteen million dollars. Would Mr. Farrell accept or pass on the proposal?

Beads of sweat formed on Johnny's forehead. His hands were clammy as he held the building's blueprints and property specifications. Fifteen million bucks. He'd never see that kind of money in a hundred lifetimes! How could Johnny authorize the sale of his benefactor's building?

Yet, Mr. Farrell had specifically instructed him to make decisions on his behalf in all business matters that were left undone. And he couldn't fail him, not after all he owed Mr. Farrell.

"Well, Mr. Farrell," the real estate broker began, "do we have a deal?"

"Let me see," Johnny pondered in what he considered was a financier's businesslike manner.

The building was only partly leased. The area reports indicated that many of the office buildings on that street were also not fully leased. Therefore, Mr. Farrell wasn't receiving the income he had projected for full occupancy. If Johnny sold the building, he'd garner a five-million-dollar profit for him.

Johnny swallowed the huge golf ball stuck in his throat. If he didn't make the deal and Mr. Farrell wished he had, he would have royally screwed up. He'd already blundered the university study for Mr. Farrell. He had to come through with this deal.

"Get the contract ready," Johnny ordered. "Let's get this deal going."

Unbeknownst to the agent, Johnny was finding it hard to breathe. Man, oh, man, he'd better be doing the right thing with Mr. Farrell's ten-million-dollar property!

The real estate broker dropped him off at Mr. Farrell's mansion, saying that his decision was a financially sound one. Maybe she was right.

Johnny couldn't help feeling a sense of accomplishment as he turned the key to open the copper double doors. Turning ten million dollars into fifteen million dollars was an incredible feat.

He went straight into the kitchen, gulped down half a container of milk from the carton and brushed off his mouth with the back of his hand. A five-million-dollar profit in one day! He couldn't get over it.

As Johnny headed toward the staircase for the master suite, he suddenly stopped in his tracks. He stared at the massive living room with its sterling-silver and crystal ornaments. What was wrong with him? He'd gotten himself so deep into Mr. Farrell's life that he was starting to actually *feel* as if he was Mr. Farrell!

A wave of nausea hit him. The truth spat in his face. Being Mr. Farrell was of unbelievable importance to him now that Rachel was in his life. He wanted her so bad that he damn wished he could become the man.

Johnny pounded up the lavender-carpeted staircase to the master suite. He angrily hurled the suit jacket and tie onto the satin-covered bed. He stared at his greasy overalls and oil-stained shirt lying on the master-bathroom floor.

He used to be proud of being Johnny Wells. Now the thought of returning to his shop, the shop he loved so much, felt second-rate to the upscale life-style he'd experienced in Mr. Farrell's world. And that realization was murdering him most of all.

* * *

Rachel sat with pad and pencil in the staid Volvo of Harvey Glitt, her accountant case study.

Harvey had requested that her interview take place in his car. He said he'd tried to reach a client about an important matter which needed resolving, but the client had not responded to any of his phone messages. Therefore, he needed to go directly to the client's house to take care of the matter. He hoped that Rachel would not mind, since he did not want to miss her interview.

Rachel agreed to his request. It was her last interview with Harvey. That didn't bother her because his study felt complete.

She'd already set up her last interview with Chester Zole to take place in a couple of weeks. But she'd purposely put off calling Zane.

She dreaded telling him that he had only one interview left with her. That it would be their last time together. She couldn't bear the thought that she'd never see him again. Because the fact was that every outing and meeting they'd spent together was under the guise of the research project. Zane had never asked her out on his own. Once she finished the project, he'd have no reason to see her again.

As Harvey Glitt drove, he abruptly turned to her in rare eye-to-eye contact.

"It—it happened, Rachel," Harvey began in a shy voice.

"What, Harvey?"

"I met a sweet lady," he replied, avoiding her eyes now. "She has said yes to every dating invitation of mine."

"That's wonderful," she told him. She knew Harvey's finding a nice woman was a large accomplishment for him since he had so little self-confidence with women.

"I attribute all of my good fortune to you, Rachel."

She was taken aback. "Why me?"

Harvey's timid voice was so low she had to strain to hear. "Discussing my lacking sex life with you has been—well— of great assistance to me," he admitted. "I feel a bit more at ease with myself. I figure maybe a woman out there might be attracted to my reserved ways. Now I met Glinda Jelson. She's the librarian at the public library I frequent every Saturday morning.''

"Oh, Harvey, I'm so happy for you!" She would've hugged him, but Harvey tensed up whenever she came closer than a foot of his physical presence.

Suddenly, Harvey turned his Volvo off Sunset Boulevard into Bel Air. Rachel immediately straightened in her seat. He stopped his car at the closed King Kong gates of Zane Farrell's property.

"What—what's the name of the client you're visiting?" she forced out.

"Zane Farrell," Harvey replied. "I have never personally met the man. We do business by fax. But in this case, I must make a personal appearance. I hope you do not mind."

"No, no, of course not."

Harvey buzzed the black security pad, and the video camera pointed in the Volvo's direction. Rachel quickly turned her face away, even though she knew only the driver could be viewed by the camera.

"Can I help you?" Zane's deep familiar voice echoed from the loudspeaker.

Rachel's hands suddenly became moist with anxiety. How could she tell Zane that they had only one more time together? She wasn't ready yet. She needed more time before her heart would be severed in half.

The King Kong gates slowly swiveled open. She held her breath as Harvey drove his Volvo onto Zane Farrell's estate.

N IMPORTANT MESSAGE
ROM THE EDITORS OF
ILHOUETTE®

ar Reader,

cause you've chosen to read one of our ne romance novels, we'd like to say hank you"! And, as a **special** way to ank you, we've selected <u>four more</u> of the oks you love so well, **and** a Cuddly ddy Bear to send you absolutely _**FREE!**_

ease enjoy them with our compliments...

Luna Macro

Senior Editor,
Silhouette Desire

P.S. And <u>because</u> we value our customers, we've attached something extra inside ...

EDITOR'S
**FREE
GIFT
SEAL**
THANK YOU

PEEL OFF SEAL AND
PLACE INSIDE

PLACE
FREE GIFT
SEAL
HERE

YES! I have placed my Editor's "thank you" seal

in the space provided above. Please send me 4 free
books and a Cuddly Teddy Bear. I understand I am under
no obligation to purchase any books, as explained on the
back and on the opposite page.

225 CIS A4UC (U-SIL-D-10/96)

_____

NAME

_____

ADDRESS   APT.

_____

CITY   STATE   ZIP

Thank you!

DETACH AND MAIL CARD TODAY!

THE SILHOUETTE READER SERVICE™: HERE'S HOW IT WORKS

Accepting free books places you under no obligation to buy anything. You may keep the books and gift and return the shipping statement marked "cancel". If you do not cancel, about a month later we will send you 6 additional novels, and bill you just $2.90 each plus 25¢ delivery and applicable sales tax, if any*. That's the complete price, and—compared to cover prices of $3.50 each—quite a bargain! You may cancel at any time, but if you choose to continue, every month we'll send you 6 more books, which you may either purchase at the discount price…or return to us and cancel your subscription.

*Terms and prices subject to change without notice. Sales tax applicable in N.Y.

Six

Johnny flicked off the intercom. It never ended! First, the real estate deal, and now an accounting problem regarding Mr. Farrell's tax records. And Johnny had just yanked on his greasy overalls and work shirt to return to his shop. He quickly telephoned Tito to let him know that he'd be back later than he wanted.

As he pulled off his coveralls and jumped back into the business suit, Johnny wanted to howl across the seas to Mr. Farrell to return to the States and handle these business matters himself. Because what if he messed up on just one business problem and financially ruined Mr. Farrell?

Johnny careened down the lavender-carpeted staircase three steps at a time. He was relieved that he'd just gone through Mr. Farrell's business records for the real estate deal. At least he was somewhat familiar with the man's holdings, and he wouldn't look like a total imbecile in front of the accountant.

As Johnny opened the front doors, he revved up a firm authoritative voice, "Mr. Glitt, I appreciate your—"

His words froze in midair when he saw Rachel standing beside the wiry accountant. What was she doing here? He could barely deal with the accountant alone, much less have the pressure of slipping up in front of Rachel.

"Mr. Farrell, this is Rachel Smith, a professor at the university doing a research study," Harvey Glitt began. "Since I am taking time away from her project to see you, I asked her to accompany me."

"Pleasure to meet you, Professor Smith," Johnny managed to say as he extended a hand to her.

"Hello, Mr. Farrell," she responded.

Her palm felt so soft in his. He wanted to pull her against his body and plant his lips on hers for a real hello. But her handshake was brief and appropriately impersonal.

Johnny's mind went into frantic motion wondering what Rachel was thinking. She hadn't called him for an interview in several days. Was it because he'd been cool to her at the end of their day together at the museum? He hadn't meant to hurt her feelings. He wanted to tell her, but Harvey Glitt was in the way.

Harvey hauled his paper-exploding briefcase into his arms and pulled out some documents.

"We must discuss this tax issue, Mr. Farrell," Harvey said.

Johnny's lungs felt on the verge of collapse. How was he going to pretend to be a financial whiz with Rachel's eyes on him? He'd have no excuse to give her for being corporate-tax ignorant.

"Maybe we should take care of the matter at a later date," Johnny suggested, glancing at his watch as though he had a zillion appointments to take care of.

"We must resolve it right now, Mr. Farrell," Harvey insisted. "If this tax situation is put aside a moment longer, you will sustain major monetary penalties from the federal government."

"Yes, of course," Johnny quickly said, not wanting to be responsible for putting Mr. Farrell into IRS hell.

As Johnny led Mr. Glitt and Rachel into Mr. Farrell's office, a veil of gray doom filled his intestines. The walls of the silver-carpeted office felt as if they were closing in on him.

Anger surged through his bloodstream. He was tired of pretending to be Mr. Farrell. He wanted to yell out to the world the damn truth about himself and break free of Mr. Farrell's identity chains.

Yet, when Rachel's brown eyes caught his, he knew she was seeing Mr. Farrell's prestige and power. And he wanted to possess those superior qualities for her. Once again, he loathed returning to the common life of Johnny Wells. He was getting more and more hooked on being Mr. Farrell, hooked real bad.

"Mr. Farrell," Rachel began, nervously clasping her hands in front of her, "would you prefer doing business alone with Mr. Glitt?"

"No, no, no," Johnny abruptly replied. He didn't want to cause any more suspicion about himself than he'd already done with the Mrs. Guillino matter. Let her feel open and free around him, as if he had nothing to hide. He turned to Harvey. "Shall we proceed?"

Rachel could feel Zane's intense gaze on her as Harvey explained the tax intricacies involved with Zane's multicorporate operations. She yearned to be alone with him. Yet, she dreaded that moment because of the horrible news she needed to tell him.

She abruptly arose from the black leather chair, unable to sit still. She peered out the picture window overlooking the mountains, not really seeing a thing but listening to their conversation.

"Mr. Farrell, if you continue to keep your apartment buildings under the umbrella of your entertainment corporation," Harvey said, "an audit might cost you hundreds of thousands of dollars in fines due to a new tax law—that is, if your venture is ever detected by the IRS."

"What are my options?" Zane inquired.

"Firstly, you could—" Harvey rambled on with boring tax talk.

In the reflection on the windowpane, Rachel could see Zane sitting at his expansive oak desk constantly looking over at her. His voice seemed unsteady. He nervously tapped a pen on the desk top. He seemed jumpy. Was her presence interfering more than he wanted to admit?

"Oh, my," Harvey said, shuffling through his briefcase. "Mr. Farrell, I am missing a recent financial statement for your entertainment corporation. I believe you failed to send a copy to my accounting office. May I see one now?"

"A financial statement?" Johnny repeated in total confusion.

Johnny frantically scrambled through the papers on Mr. Farrell's desk. Sheets were flying to the floor. He didn't remember seeing a financial statement for the entertainment corporation when he'd sifted through Mr. Farrell's business files.

"Is something wrong, Mr. Farrell?" Harvey asked.

"Not at all," Johnny told him.

"We need that statement," Harvey went on.

"I know it's alive under all these papers," Johnny said.

Johnny noticed Rachel turn to face him. He was sure she sensed that something was off. He couldn't blow the whole thing now over a scrap of paper!

Johnny forced a smile to Rachel. "So many corporations and so little time," he joked, trying to stay in focus but needing to find a solution fast.

"Can I help you?" Rachel asked, her eyebrows curled into a frown.

"Don't worry, I'll find the statement," Johnny insisted, totally worried out of his head.

He frantically opened and closed the drawers of Mr. Farrell's desk searching for the damn thing.

Just then, Harvey Glitt's beeper went off. "Please excuse me," Harvey said and then put himself into a more private setting in another room to make a call.

Rachel walked over to Johnny. "Is there a problem?" she asked.

Johnny was practically yanking out every folder in the file cabinet to find that paper.

"Heck, no," Johnny quickly assured her. "With my secretary on vacation, I'm lost."

"I can help if you want," she said. "Should I look in this drawer?" She put her hand on the handle ready to open it.

"No!" Johnny said, grabbing her hand. He wasn't sure what she'd find that might unveil the truth about him.

"Zane, are you okay?" she asked in a worried voice.

"Yeah, sure," he said.

"I'm sorry I'm here with Harvey," she went on. "I know it's making you tense with your business—"

"I'm not sorry," Johnny cut in, still holding on to her hand.

"You're not?" she asked, her brown eyes gazing into his without an ounce of resistance in them.

He interlaced his fingers with hers and squeezed. The electricity thundered straight to his loins.

"If we can think of a way of getting rid of Glitt—" Johnny began, just wanting to think of her and forget the financial statement, the tax problem, Harvey Glitt—

Harvey abruptly returned to the room. "Did you find the statement, Mr. Farrell?" he asked.

"It's almost at my fingertips," Johnny said, immediately releasing Rachel's hand.

"If you will excuse me," Rachel said. "I'll only be a moment."

Rachel closed the door to the powder room. She peered at her flushed face in the diamond-shaped mirror.

Zane's electric gaze and his fingers intertwining with hers had heated her skin to boiling point. The tender area between her thighs still pulsated from the steam of his eyes. She wasn't winning this battle with herself. She was losing it!

As she dabbed cool water on her cheeks, there was something else that disturbed her. It was the uneasy way Zane was handling Harvey's visit.

It seemed strange that he didn't know where his important financial papers were. A man of his super intelligence and mogul status had to be intricately aware of every facet of his billion-dollar enterprise. Yet, Zane had seemed confused, unsure, even nervous about the answers he needed to give Harvey. Why did she still have a sense that he was hiding something?

Johnny breathed easily as Harvey looked over the statements he'd finally found under a pile of Mr. Farrell's untouched mail.

"All there, right?" Johnny asked, leaning back with relief in Mr. Farrell's black leather chair.

"Seems to be," Harvey replied. "Now I need to know what you want to do about the apartment-building-expense write-offs. Do I keep them with the same corporation?"

"Let's see," Johnny reluctantly said. He only knew about writing off car-repair expenses on his tax forms. He knew nothing of billion-dollar-corporation stuff. What the hell answer was he going to give Glitt?

As he frustratingly pondered what to do, Rachel returned to the room. Her cheeks were rosy-red. Her eyes glittered. He wanted to shoo Harvey away and be cozily alone with her. But instead, he had to act like a clever financier so she wouldn't detect anything off about him.

Harvey Glitt was waiting for an answer.

"All right, all right," Johnny said abruptly. "Switch the apartments from the entertainment corporation to one of my real estate companies. I think that'll take care of the IRS problem." At least, he hoped to hell it would.

"It is done, Mr. Farrell," Harvey said, zipping up his briefcase, shaking Johnny's hand and heading out the office door.

Before Rachel could follow, Johnny grabbed her hand to stop her. He needed to be alone with her for just a few more seconds.

"When do I see you again?" he asked.

"Zane," she said, her voice straining, "I only have one more interview with you."

"What do you mean?" Johnny asked, feeling his heart being snapped in two.

"The research study is near completion," she explained. "My job is almost over."

"It can't be," he said, running his fingers through his hair, trying to find a way out.

"Rachel, coming?" Harvey called from downstairs.

Johnny felt a frantic need to keep Rachel there with him and never let her go.

"Rachel, I—" Johnny stopped midsentence. He wanted to tell her feelings he knew he had no place telling her. "I'll have a cab pick you up Friday morning."

"Where will it take me?"

Johnny's idea was crazy. But he was a desperate man now—desperate to extend his last few hours with her for as long as he could.

"It's a surprise," Johnny replied.

Her lips tenderly brushed against Johnny's mouth and then she rushed out to join Harvey Glitt downstairs.

Leaving Zane was like setting her heart on the floor and walking out the door.

On the way back with Harvey, Rachel could barely remember asking him her last research question. When he dropped her off at the university, she warmly thanked him for his help in the study and wished him luck in his new relationship with the librarian.

She rushed out of his Volvo, desperately needing to be alone. Once inside the building, she walked toward her office in a daze. A rush of students passed her in the hallway saying hello, but she didn't see any of them.

She just had one final interview with Zane. She couldn't bear the idea that Zane Farrell would be out of her life for good.

Johnny zipped his pickup into the shop in seconds flat. Tito was waiting for him with a handful of customer problems. As Johnny summoned the solutions, he hoped the tax decision he'd given Harvey Glitt on behalf of Mr. Farrell was the right one. In his gut, he felt it was, and that was all he could go by.

As Johnny talked cars with a customer, his mind was plagued with the frustration of where to reach Mr. Farrell in Paris. Why did the man have to be so remote and private? Johnny only had one day left to spend with Rachel. Couldn't it be an honest one?

Yet, Johnny knew the devastating answer. If he wanted to continue seeing Rachel after the university study was over, he'd have to be Mr. Farrell to do so, not Johnny Wells. Should he keep up the front just to keep seeing her—at least until Mr. Farrell got back?

His thoughts continued to torment him later as he jammed a wrench inside a sooty black engine. He knew he couldn't deliberately lie to her outside of Mr. Farrell's commitment to the university project. But he was determined about one thing. He was going to make her last interview a very special one. And he'd do it Zane Farrell–style all the way.

* * *

Early that morning, Rachel's apartment doorbell rang exactly the time Zane had promised. She peeked out the front window and saw a yellow taxi waiting to pick her up.

A surge of excited anticipation shot through her as she gathered her leather briefcase and jingling keys. She couldn't wait to see Zane. But her enthusiasm was immediately tempered when she reminded herself that this might be their last day together.

Johnny raced Mr. Farrell's red Porsche into the Santa Monica Airport parking lot. As he parked the car, he dialed Tito from the car phone.

"Any word from Mr. Farrell?" Johnny asked hopefully.

"*Nada*," Tito replied. "But if he calls, I will forward him to you."

"Thanks, Tito." Disappointed for the zillionth time, Johnny clicked off the cellular and hopped out of the Porsche.

The morning wind hit Johnny's clean-shaven face as the air current blew across the open airport field. His adrenaline fired up when he spotted Mr. Farrell's blue-and-white private jet. The pilot Johnny had hired in Mr. Farrell's name was checking one of the engines.

Before Mr. Farrell had left for his world trip, he'd told Johnny that he could call a licensed pilot and fly his privately owned jet whenever he desired. Mr. Farrell insisted that Johnny also arrange for a butler to be on board. Johnny decided that this was the time to take up Mr. Farrell on his offer. Only, Johnny was paying for every cent of it out of his own savings.

As Johnny shook hands with the pilot, his eyes locked on Rachel climbing out of the yellow cab. Her chestnut tresses blew back from her ivory face as she walked toward him with twinkling eyes. Her pink summer dress pasted against the contours of her thighs indenting the triangular shape between her legs.

Johnny's breath caught as he watched her full breasts bob up and down beneath her top with each step. He could barely hear the pilot say that he was going into the cockpit to get ready for takeoff.

Rachel quickened her pace toward Zane. She wanted to fling herself into Zane's arms and go off into that jet together forever.

"Zane!" Rachel called out with utter joy just to see him again. "Is this your plane?"

"Ready to go for a ride?" Zane asked, taking her hand in his.

"Right now?" she asked in disbelief. Did his sea-blues hold a yearning as he looked at her? Was he thinking about future days with her which were not part of the study? She couldn't tell.

"The pilot's ready to leave whenever we are," Zane said as he led her up the steps into his private jet.

Her eyes widened with wonder as she entered. The interior had exquisite royal-blue carpeting, a plush snow-white sofa and walnut coffee table bolted to the floor. She felt as if she were on the presidential jet.

"Where are you taking me?" she asked, not that she cared at all. He could take her straight to the rings of Saturn and she'd be thrilled just being with him.

She settled down on the white sofa, and Zane sat right beside her. She wanted to hug him and kiss him and tell him—

"We're going to Enseneda," Zane said.

"Mexico?" she repeated incredulously.

"Is that okay?" Zane asked, a bit concerned. "If you'd rather stay in L.A. for the interview—"

"No, no!" she quickly said. "Mexico sounds perfect."

"I knew you'd feel that way," he said with an irresistible grin.

Just then, a butler entered with a tray of wineglasses filled with freshly squeezed orange juice, croissants of all flavors, jams of strawberry, peach and apricot, and fresh-brewed mocha java coffee.

The moment the butler left, Rachel stared at Zane. He was sitting close to her on the white sofa. Her thigh was pressed against his muscled one. She tried to memorize every laugh line, every curl in his hair. It didn't have to end between them. All he had to do was say the word. And she wouldn't hesitate a second to say yes, she'd see him every day if he wanted.

"I wish the university study could last for ten more years," she heard herself say. She knew she shouldn't have admitted her longing, but she needed to let him know that she was there, if he wanted her.

"Me, too," he said with sadness in his voice.

Why didn't he say that their relationship could go on? She wished she could do something that would make him see that she wanted to be with him beyond the project—way beyond.

Just then, the butler returned with a tray filled with heated cinnamon and walnut danish. Rachel felt in turmoil as she glanced at Zane, trying to figure out exactly what he was feeling about her.

Zane's private jet arrived in Mexico so quickly that she realized she hadn't even started the final part of her interview. She knew why. Asking him that last question would be the end of their sharing, the end of the greatest happiness she'd ever felt in her entire life.

Upon disembarking from Mr. Farrell's jet, Johnny hailed a Mexican cab as though he knew exactly where he was going. Was he trying to impress Rachel? Hell, yes, he was. He had one last chance to be the man he wished he could be in her life.

Thanks to Tito's last-minute coaching, Johnny could even speak some coherent Spanish with the cabdriver. Also, be-

fore he'd left L.A., he'd scoured through the rest of Mr.
Farrell's files at the Bel Air mansion and found a list of his
benefactor's favorite restaurants in Enseneda.

The treasure of it all was that Mr. Farrell had a private
cabana on a sandy Mexican beach, furnished with beach
towels and swimsuits of all sizes for his guests.

Yes, Johnny had come fully prepared for Mexico and his
last official time as Mr. Farrell with Professor Rachel Smith.
But he wasn't prepared for the hurricane of unrest he felt
knowing he was only Johnny Wells.

The cab stopped in front of the Sanchez Restaurant. Before Rachel followed Zane inside, he stopped walking and
looked a bit worried.

"I forgot to ask," Zane began. "I hope you like Mexican food."

"I hate it," she said, staring at him very seriously like how
dare you take me to a place without asking first.

"Oh, man, I'm in trouble now," Zane said, nervously
running his fingers through his curls.

She couldn't help breaking out into a giggle. "Got you."

"Don't worry, I'll have my turn," Zane said.

Zane slipped an arm possessively around her, pulled her
tightly against him and led her into the restaurant. She
warmed inside as his hand soothingly caressed her back as
they were directed to a table, as if they were really together
inside.

Lively Mexican guitar music filled her ears. Rainbow
paintings of famous Mexican conquerors on the walls
caught her eye.

Zane chose a cozy booth in a private corner. Rachel
struggled with the knowledge that even though deep down
she felt like a real couple with him, their closeness would
only exist for a few more precious hours.

She couldn't even remember what she ate, maybe a que-
sadilla, cheese enchilada or a chicken taco. How could she

think of her stomach? Zane's eyes never left hers, as though he was mesmerized by her, and she by him.

"Zane, tell me all about your family," she said, dying to learn every morsel about his life from birth to right that very moment.

Johnny nearly coughed up his margarita. "Didn't the university do any research about my life before choosing me for the study?"

"Of course," she replied, dipping a chip into the spicy salsa.

"So what did you find out about me?"

"Nothing," she stated, frowning. "For some reason, no one could find any facts on your family background."

"With all the potential media problems," Johnny quickly said, "I prefer keeping my personal life well-concealed from the public."

"Does that include me?" She leaned forward on the small table. Her rosebud lips were so close that he couldn't resist outlining her soft bottom lip with his thumb.

Her lips parted, and he slipped his finger into her mouth. Her eyes never left his. He felt her tongue gently lick his thumb.

Rachel's breathing quickened as Zane's finger lingered in her mouth. She wanted to stay calm and unaffected. But she lightly bit the skin of his thumb, and when he sucked in his breath, her body throbbed with desire.

Luckily, the waiter walked over to take their dessert order. Like she wasn't already having dessert! Zane gently withdrew his finger from her mouth and began talking to the waiter in Spanish.

Rachel excused herself and escaped into the ladies' room to recover. She redid her red lipstick with trembling fingers. Her forehead was aching. Her temperature was feverish.

Stay in control, she cautioned herself. *If you release your unbridled fire, you'll scare him off forever.*

In the back seat of the taxi with Zane's arm around her shoulders, he could have been taking her to Zambia for all she cared. She rested her head against his broad shoulder. She gently rubbed his muscled thigh with her hand. She could see the bulge under his pants growing, and she ached to inch her palm up and caress his manhood. But she firmly kept her hand in place.

Johnny could barely remember paying the cabdriver. His heart was hammering against his rib cage. His body was acutely aroused. He knew he should take Rachel back to Santa Monica Airport immediately. But he wasn't following his logical mind anymore.

With her hand in his, he led her through a lush green path in what he hoped was the direction of the cabana. He followed his instincts as per the pictures he'd seen in Mr. Farrell's file.

Suddenly, a cozy cabana appeared, a white sandy beach and turquoise ocean for a backyard.

"Zane, it's—it's magnificent!"

"It sure is!" Johnny exclaimed, amazed at the shimmering beauty of the place. Then he quickly sobered up to his role. "I knew you'd like it."

Johnny nervously unlocked the front door with the key Mr. Farrell had left for him at his Bel Air house. The living room was decorated with Oriental rugs, a fireplace, and flowered sofa and love seat. He prayed she wouldn't ask where the bathroom was.

To his relief, Rachel immediately went exploring on her own. She disappeared into another room.

"I think there are swimsuits somewhere," Johnny called out as he rushed around surveying the place, trying to memorize the details in case she asked. He remembered Mr. Farrell telling him not to worry about any personal photos lying around to destroy his role-playing, in case he wanted to take a female guest there.

"I found the bathing suits," Rachel yelled back from the other room. "I'll get one for you, too."

Rachel was astonished at the drawerful of designer spandex swimsuits in the large bedroom. She stuck her head out the door and flung Zane a pair of brief green swim trunks.

"I'll change in here," she told him. Then she closed the bedroom door. Her breathing was erratic as she stared at the enticing gold bikini she'd picked out.

She shed her clothes, and standing naked in front of the full-length mirror, she slipped on the scanty top and bottom. She gasped at her reflection.

Her breasts spilled out of the skimpy gold held up by a flimsy string around her neck and a string behind her back. The gold triangular patch barely covered her.

Had she lost her mind? If she wanted to keep sensual feelings to a minimum, why had she turned up the volume? She knew she should put her own clothes back on, ask Zane the final research question and escape to her safe apartment in Los Angeles.

But she couldn't run away from him now. Not when her entire being was crying out to get closer to him.

Rachel nervously opened the bedroom door and walked into the living room in the gold bikini with breathless anticipation of his response.

But the cabana was quiet, except for the lapping of waves in the distance.

"Zane?" she called.

No answer. She noticed the back door was open onto the beach. She stepped outside to find him.

The hot sun instantly heated the expanse of her flesh. Squinting her eyes in the brightness, she saw a red blanket lying on the sand. Then she spotted Zane diving into a swirling ocean wave.

Johnny's body shot through the curl of the wave then arose to the surface in the deep sea. He immediately began to swim. The cold salty ocean chilled down his burning skin from the memories of Rachel's body near his.

Johnny knew he had to keep control of himself. He was still representing Mr. Farrell. He had to be sure to keep the man's impressive reputation intact on the final university interview. He couldn't let the Johnny Well's side of him take over.

Johnny glided through the choppy sea. Back in the cabana while Rachel was slipping on her swimsuit, he'd telephoned his shop. Johnny's heart had dropped to the cabana floor. Tito said that Mr. Farrell had called only minutes before. Tito suggested Mr. Farrell immediately phone his private jet or the cabana in Mexico to find Johnny.

But Mr. Farrell had called Tito back to say that he couldn't locate Johnny in the jet or cabana. Johnny knew he'd either been at the Mexican restaurant or in the taxi.

Tito said he tried to get Mr. Farrell's phone number. But Mr. Farrell was on the move again and promised to try Johnny another time.

Torn apart with frustration, Johnny pounded his strokes even harder against the vibrant sea. Though his mind demanded that he reach Mr. Farrell, the part of him that was falling hard for Rachel never wanted to connect with Mr. Farrell again. He secretly wished he could keep Rachel in that Mexican cabana and never return to his Johnny Wells world again.

Johnny was pushing so hard through the surf his arms began to tire. Just as he reached shallower water, he heard Rachel's voice calling out to him over the crashing waves.

Johnny spotted her running into the ocean in a glittery gold bikini. Her full breasts exploded over the skimpy top. As the seawater splashed against the gold fabric, her nipples hardened and protruded through the thin material. When she turned against a wave, her glitter gold barely concealed her naked round buttocks.

Johnny felt his cooled-down body fire up like a lit barbecue. Did she have to torpedo his libido every time?

"Zane!" she yelled as she splashed into the waves toward him.

Just then, a gigantic breaker appeared like a monstrous wall in front of her and crashed down with such force that she was gobbled up by the torrential water. She suddenly disappeared from the sea's surface.

"Rachel!" Johnny screamed.

He powered his strokes toward her, cutting through the ocean at shark speed. He saw her struggle to arise only to be shoved back underwater by another wave.

He knew he had to reach her before the riptide pulled her back out into the depths of the ocean. He felt his feet touch the sandy bottom. He ran toward her, gasping for breath as the breaking waves twisted and pushed him around.

Under the swishing white water, he spotted her gold-bikinied body tumbling underwater. He grabbed her by the waist and pulled her above water into the fresh air.

"Rachel, Rachel," Johnny whispered as she coughed and spewed out the salty liquid.

"Zane," she said in a choked voice and then collapsed in his arms.

Johnny lifted her wet body in his arms and rushed her to shore. He kissed her cheek and held her close to keep her warm.

"Rachel, Rachel," he kept saying over and over. "If anything ever happened to you—"

His words stopped him cold. He knew their untold meaning. And he also knew the inevitable doom that would follow once his true identity was revealed.

Johnny gently laid her down on the red blanket on the sand. She was breathing okay, and her eyelids slowly opened. When she saw it was him, a tiny smile crossed her lips.

An audible sigh escaped from Johnny's lips, and he rubbed her cold hands.

"You're okay, Rachel. You're okay."

She barely nodded and then momentarily closed her eyes to rest.

Johnny knew she was exhausted. He stroked her hands between his palms to get them warm. She was all right, that's all that mattered to him.

It wasn't until Johnny's frantic need to get her out of the ocean to safety was over that he noticed that the flimsy string of her bikini top had come loose. The glittering gold had slipped down, and her swelling bare breasts were heaving with each breath she took.

Johnny's hands stopped massaging hers. His gaze was riveted to the fullness just inches from his touch. Her nipples were button-hard from the icy seawater.

Pull her top back up! Johnny warned himself. He hesitantly touched the gold material lying under her naked mounds. *Cover them!* his inner voice screamed out. But his fingers remained frozen on the fabric as he fought the desire to squeeze her nude breasts and press his bare eager palms against her taut nipples.

Against his sexual will, Johnny forced his resistant fingers to begin lifting the skimpy gold fabric. Just as he was about to cover her naked globes with the glittering fabric, her eyes opened.

Rachel saw Zane's face above hers as she heard the rush of crashing waves. His eyes were glazed, his lips parted.

She saw his fingers clutching her gold bikini top. Her breathing quickened when she realized he was taking off her top to reveal her breasts.

She should have sat up and covered herself. Instead, she lay still with his massive hands barely touching her now-throbbing breasts.

"Your—your top fell down," Zane began in a gravelly voice. "I was just lifting it—"

Zane's moist muscular chest revealed his excited rapid breathing.

Rachel's gaze unconsciously slid down to his brief green trunks. She could see the clear outline of his manhood straining against the wet elastic fabric. She felt a quivering under the miniature patch covering the pleasure zone between her thighs.

Her heart was thumping as she lay there all open and vulnerable to him under the hot Mexican sun.

Zane's fingertips touched her naked nipples. He leaned his head down over her bosom and slipped a perky nipple between his lips.

Rachel should have stopped him, just to let herself and him know that she had control. But she couldn't contain her own pent-up impulses. Instead, she arched her back to him in response to his passion. His hands clutched her back and pushed her pulsating breasts farther inside his mouth.

She moaned as his tongue licked and sucked one hard knob and then slid across her chest to the other taut tip.

A low groan came from the depths of Zane's throat as he nuzzled his face between her cleavage and pressed both breasts against his cheeks feeling the warmth of her.

She clutched his wet curly hair in response to the ecstasy of his touch. The beach sun burned on her face as intense rainbow currents splintered every nerve in her body.

Johnny forgot about being Mr. Farrell. He forgot about restraining Johnny Wells. Rachel was responding to him as if he was everything to her. And there was no way he could hold back the fiery desire he'd felt for her for so long.

He was Johnny Wells now—through and through—tasting the swollen flesh of her. Johnny nibbled on the hill of her breasts as if it were needed food for his being, and Rachel moaned in response.

With a zealousness he couldn't repress, Johnny slid his tongue down her hot silken breasts to her flat abdomen. His fingers slipped under the waist string of her gold bikini bottom and pulled the scanty fabric down her bare thighs.

Johnny heard her suck in her breath as he freed her feminine area to the sea air. Her chestnut patch of pleasure temptingly gleamed out at him. He felt his manhood respond at the sensual sight of her.

Johnny's brain immediately registered a warning signal. His mind ordered him to stop. But yearning to get closer to her, to taste her womanliness, he didn't listen. He parted her naked legs and kissed the tender flesh of her thighs. Then he fulfilled his deepest desire to become even more intimate with her.

Rachel held her breath as Zane tenderly explored her most private area. Her fingers tightened around the curls of his moist black hair letting him know she wanted him to taste of her.

"Zane, oh, Zane!" she called out, her ecstatic moans echoing across the expansive beach.

Her thighs parted farther to allow him even closer to her. She wanted him to know her in secret ways that nobody else did.

Suddenly, she heard the roar of a helicopter in the distance. The roar got louder and louder as the helicopter neared their naked bodies on the beach, but she ignored it and succumbed to the passion of their act.

But as the helicopter flew directly above them, she became startlingly aware of her bare arched body pressed against Zane.

Her eyes shot open. Her thinking became shamefully crystal-clear. She was appalled at herself. She wiggled free of Zane's mouth and fondling hands. With trembling fingers, she grasped the gold bikini top and bottom from the sand and scrambled naked off the blanket.

"Rachel!" Zane called in a hoarse voice.

But Rachel didn't stop. She ran toward the cabana clutching the bikini pieces to her breasts, feeling unbearably ashamed. She tripped and fell into the sand but pulled herself back up, feeling agonizingly humiliated by her blatant, glaring obsessed need for him.

Seven

Rachel closed the door to the cabana bedroom. The bikini pieces dropped from her numb fingertips to the floor. Her skin was sweltering from the passion of Zane's body on hers. Her bare breasts and nipples were pounding with desire. The feminine area between her thighs was throbbing and moist from Zane's intimate touch.

Just thinking about his lips on her femininity caused a contraction of pleasure to erupt through her every muscle.

Stop it! Stop it! she mentally screamed at her overly titillated body. *You're going to lose him!*

Zane was so part of her heart now, she felt tears rushing to her eyes. When he'd carried her out of the rough sea in his arms, she was barely conscious but could feel him kiss her gently on the cheek. She'd heard him whisper her name over and over, and she knew he cared—he cared a lot.

She didn't want to push him out of her life. She couldn't let her unbridled sexual nature frighten him away.

Her trembling, pulsating body ached to go back out on the beach with him. But her mind said no. *He cares for you now,* her brain echoed. *Don't ruin it!*

Suddenly, there was a knock at the bedroom door. Without waiting for her to respond, the door swung open Zane Farrell–style.

Zane stood there in his damp green swim trunks holding a small object in his hand. His sensual gaze caressed her naked flesh. His bronzed chest heaved with each rapid breath.

His sea-blues met hers with yearning, with a need to complete what they'd started.

Rachel's limbs felt like putty. She didn't hide her bare breasts. She didn't cover her naked femininity with her palms. She stood in front of Zane with her skin flaming red-hot from his bold stare.

"Zane," she whispered.

Without a word, Zane stepped toward her. His eyes were set on her mouth. Her desire for him was so strong, so overwhelming she knew she couldn't restrain herself.

The sheer nearness of his pulsating masculine body compelled her to forget all the vows she'd made to herself. She wanted him fully. No mental chains or restrictions would hold her back from fulfilling her deepest yearning to be physically one with him.

Zane's mouth covered hers as though those few moments from the beach to the cabana had been a torturous eternity. He drew her naked body against his muscled chest. Whatever was in his palm fell to the floor. He stroked the length of her bare back as if he were touching velvet. His palms felt warm on her buttocks, and she pressed herself closer against his maleness under his swim trunks.

Rachel's body throbbed with an inner desire to know Zane as intimately as he had dared to know her on the beach. She was aroused, so excited, so intensely caught up in him that she didn't worry about what he might think of her.

She clutched his powerful back muscles and slid her trembling fingers to the elastic waistband of his swim trunks. She slowly nudged down the fabric and let it drop to the floor.

As Zane nibbled at her earlobe, he kicked his trunks across the room.

Rachel gently slid her lips down Zane's neck and across the curly hairs of his chest. She tasted the salty seawater on his tanned skin.

Rachel couldn't stop herself. She *wouldn't* stop herself. As her mouth slowly moved farther down his body, she felt Zane's breathing quicken.

She let go, let go, and there was no holding back. His manliness immediately responded as she tasted his most private area. She felt close to him, so close to him. His fingers slid through her hair, letting her know he felt close to her, too.

Her hands gripped the backs of his muscled thighs. He quivered and shuddered at the movements of her mouth. His fingers gripped the strands of her hair more tightly. He groaned out loud, and his pleasurable response excited her to quicken her motions.

Just as he reached explosive proportions, he gently released her from him. Breathing unevenly, he laid her nakedness onto the carpeted floor.

Rachel opened her arms to him, desperately needing him, wanting him to become one with her. Zane picked up the condom he'd brought into the room and slipped it on. Then his sea-blues momentarily locked with hers in an intimate visual embrace, and he merged his body with hers.

"Zane!" Rachel cried out in ultimate ecstasy.

She accepted him deeper into her femininity, fulfilling the intense desire she'd felt for so long. His sensual movements were steady, rhythmic, sending untold heights of pleasure through her every nerve. She moaned out loud not caring who in the universe heard her.

She circled her legs around his waist, moving in total harmony with him as though they had made love for aeons. She squeezed her legs tighter around him as electrical sensations flooded her limbs. Orgasmic spasms radiated through her again and again and again as she responded to his every sensual thrust.

"Rachel, I need you!" Zane groaned in her ear as his muscles tensed up to an uncontrolled peak.

His manhood swelled and swelled inside her until he finally exploded. Rainbow lights filled her head. Sparks of pleasure massaged every inch of her skin as she clutched him closer to her.

Her body slowly relaxed, and her breathing eased. Rachel lay beside Zane on the carpeted floor feeling a soothing coat of contentment cover her entire being. She could hear the crashing ocean waves from the open window. A cool breeze of salty air drifted onto her damp skin. She felt a peacefulness enter her soul like the soft stroke of an angel's wing.

"Zane," she whispered. "I never felt so—"

Zane abruptly slipped free of her and arose from the floor. Without a word, he turned his back and slipped on his swim trunks, seeming distant, remote.

A pain seared through Rachel like a sharp kitchen knife digging into her heart. It was Kent all over again. But now the nightmare was with the man she desired most.

Swallowing back the sob in her throat, Rachel stood up. Her legs felt wobbly. Her head was pounding.

"I'm sorry we didn't make it to the interview," she forced herself to say to Zane, his back still toward her. She struggled to get her clothes on. "But—but I've got all the information I need now."

Zane didn't say a word. Starting to shiver, she sat on the bed and reached for her sandals. Her hands were trembling so much she could barely hold the shoe. She struggled to put one sandal on, when she realized she was putting her left sandal on her right foot. Angry and hurt, she hurled the shoe to the floor fighting back sobs.

"Rachel," Zane said as he went to her side and gently touched her shoulder.

"You don't have to avoid the issue!" she said in a choked voice. "I already know my weakness. And now you know, too."

He took both her hands in his and tugged her to her feet.

"What are you talking about?" he firmly asked.

She pulled free of him and grabbed her left sandal to put it on. But Zane took hold of her hand to stop her.

"Tell me!" he demanded, forcing her to look him straight in the eye.

"You turned cold after we made love," she managed to say. "I know exactly how you feel about our lovemaking."

"No, Rachel, no," Zane said. "It wasn't because of you. My mind drifted to something else—something I'll never be able to solve." He grabbed her by the shoulders. "Rachel, I didn't mean to hurt you. Making love to you was the greatest thing that's ever happened to me."

"It was?" she asked, desperately wanting to believe his words.

"Can't you see how I feel about you?" he said, gently pulling her to him.

"You're not turned off by me?" she asked, her voice shaking, her heart open and feeling so very vulnerable.

"Turned off?" Zane repeated incredulously. "Oh, Rachel, Rachel!" He nuzzled his lips to her ear. "You're every fantasy I've ever had about a woman."

Rachel blinked back the tears that were clouding her vision. She looked deeply into his sea-blues searching for the truth.

"Do you mean it, Zane?" she asked. "Do you really mean it? I've already lost one man because of the way I am."

"What way?" Zane asked, sounding confused.

"My obsession with sex!" she blurted out. Then she told Zane every horrible, hurtful, humiliating thing that Kent had told her about being oversexed. It felt so good letting the words out—so freeing—as if she was cleansing her insides pure white.

After she finished, Zane gently put the palm of his hand at the back of her head and leaned her face protectively against his broad chest.

"I love your sexuality," he whispered into her hair. "Your amorous way turns me on. You're perfect, Rachel, perfect."

"Really, Zane?" she whispered with hope in her heart. She nuzzled her face against his muscular chest. She could hear his heart pounding in unison with hers, as though they were sharing one heart, one mind. She tightened her arms around his waist, feeling secure in a way she'd never dreamed she'd feel after what had happened with Kent. She was so happy Zane was in her life! So very, very happy!

As Johnny felt Rachel's arms tighten around him, he realized he never wanted to let go of her. He wanted to protect her from ever being hurt again. He wanted—

Then his senses returned.

What the hell was he doing? She was falling for Mr. Farrell, the Bel Air mansion, Mexican cabana, private jet, red convertible Porsche, and genius IQ.

You've got nothing to offer her! Johnny mentally screamed out to himself. *Nothing!*

He reached around his back, released Rachel's hands from his body and squeezed them together in front of him. Her gentle chestnut eyes looked up at him so trustingly, so lovingly. His insides wrenched with the pain of ugly deceit.

"Rachel," he began, "if I'm not the person you think I am—"

"I don't care who you are!" she cut in with a warm smile beaming on her beautiful face. "I only care about us!"

She stood on tiptoe and pressed her lips against Johnny's mouth. "Thanks for accepting me totally—completely."

Before Johnny could say another word, she kissed him again and again until he was oozing with desire again. He pulled her down to the floor and made love to her all over again.

At windy Santa Monica Airport, Mr. Farrell's private jet landed. Johnny was filled with turmoil as Rachel clung to him before she left. He felt closer to her than he could imagine feeling with any woman. Yet, he couldn't have her.

"I have all the answers I need for your sex study," Rachel whispered.

"But you never finished asking the questions," Johnny said.

"Personal experience gave me all the answers I need," she replied, kissing him on the lips. "Will you call me, Zane? I want you to."

Johnny should have told her he might, but couldn't promise, and just end it right there. But he couldn't do it. Not only because he couldn't hurt her with rejection right after she'd bared her deepest inner fear to him, but because he desperately didn't want to let her go.

"Sure," Johnny heard himself say in a faraway voice. "I'll call."

Late that evening, Rachel settled under the cozy cotton sheets of her bed, sighing with utter contentment. She'd unleashed her overzealous sexual desires and Zane had loved it!

Her lips slid into a smile as she stared at the fluttering night shadows on the ceiling of her bedroom. She'd never fall asleep. She was too ecstatically happy. All she thought about was seeing Zane again. Only this time, it wouldn't be under the guise of the university sex study.

She was going to spend time with Zane Farrell because she cared about him more than any human being in her entire life. And for the first time since Kent, she knew she could feel serious about a man again. Zane had given her that hope. And to top it off, even though it wasn't a priority of hers, Zane was one of the richest, most prestigious men in the country. She couldn't believe her luck.

It was the urgency in Tito's wide eyes that sent Johnny rushing into his shop office.

Tito immediately handed Johnny the telephone and quickly left the office, closing the door behind him.

"Johnny, I am at a hotel in Paris for a business conference," the familiar long-awaited voice of Mr. Farrell said over the invisible fiber optics. "Only a few associates in the States know of my presence here. Please forgive my delay in calling you back. It has been most hectic."

"Mr. Farrell!" Johnny said excitedly into the phone. He plopped into the old wooden chair at his desk. "Just the man I want to talk to!"

"I do hope my business matters are sitting well with you," Mr. Farrell said.

"Sure, sure, Mr. Farrell," Johnny quickly replied. He told Mr. Farrell about the real estate venture and the accountant's visit to his house in Bel Air. Then he waited with anxious anticipation, hoping he'd made the right moves for him.

"Most excellent," Mr. Farrell told Johnny. "Your decisions are quite pleasing to my ear."

"You're kidding!" Johnny said in disbelief.

"I commend you most heartily." Mr. Farrell said. "You have spared my business a great deal of financial loss and have created much monetary gain. I knew you were capable, Johnny Wells."

Johnny's heart momentarily glowed. Mr. Farrell could do that to him. Mr. Farrell—who felt almost like the father he'd lost.

"Mr. Farrell, there's one more thing," Johnny began. He took a grand breath of oxygen. "It's that university research you volunteered for. I don't think I represented you as well as you might like."

"What project?" Mr. Farrell inquired.

"That sexuality study."

"I have no notion of what you are referring to, Johnny," he said. "Maybe if you explain further, I might recognize it."

"Yes, yes, of course," Johnny said. Mr. Farrell had the world's business circuiting through his brain, so the university study wouldn't capture his attention. "Remember when you sent your résumé on-line to the university to volunteer for their sexuality-study interviews?"

"They didn't contact you, did they?" Mr. Farrell asked in a surprised tone.

"Actually, Mr. Farrell," Johnny hesitantly said, "I've been giving interviews to a female professor on your behalf." His greasy hands were sweating as he gripped the phone. "But I let the matter get out of hand."

"What are you saying, Johnny?"

"While being you, I got personally involved with the professor."

The phone line became deathly quiet. Johnny knew he was sunk. He'd wrecked Mr. Farrell's reputation at the university. He deserved whatever retribution Mr. Farrell had in mind.

Suddenly, Mr. Farrell broke into uproarious laughter in Johnny's ear.

"Mr. Farrell?" Johnny asked, unsure what was so funny since the bleakness of the situation was torturous to him.

"I am truly sorry for my inappropriate behavior," Mr. Farrell said between chuckles. "However, the matter is quite amusing to me."

"Amusing?" Johnny repeated, not understanding. The old wooden office chair squeaked as he moved to the edge and pressed the receiver hard against his ear. "I don't understand, Mr. Farrell."

"I did not volunteer for a sexuality study," Mr. Farrell told him.

"But the university has your résumé to prove it."

"I understand," Mr. Farrell told him. "However, I did not send it to them. This matter is due to the error of my butler, Martin. He indicated to me before I left on this trip that while using my computer to E-mail my résumé to a client, he inadvertently E-mailed it to the university. I certainly did not guess that my name would be mistakenly put on a sex-study list."

Mr. Farrell continued to chuckle with great amusement at the situation.

"You *never* volunteered?" Johnny said abruptly, standing up and kicking the wooden chair out of his way. He never had to pretend to be Mr. Farrell with Rachel? He could have been honest right from the start?

"I hope I have not inconvenienced you," Mr. Farrell began. "Please hold on a moment, Johnny." Johnny heard a female voice in the background. Then Mr. Farrell added, "You must forgive my ending our conversation. I am currently in Paris staying with a longtime lady friend of mine, a wonderful Frenchwoman. She has consented to return to Los Angeles with me very shortly. I shall see you soon, Johnny."

"When will you be coming back?" Johnny asked, but Mr. Farrell's line disconnected.

Johnny didn't remember putting down the phone. His black oil-stained hands clutched the edge of his desk. He'd deceived Rachel for nothing! Nothing!

His head felt as if it was about to split apart. He yanked open the office door, seeing red. He was relieved that Tito was busy with a customer. He didn't want to talk. He didn't want to breathe.

In a fury, he returned to rotating tires on his customer's car. He angrily yanked off one of the tires and dropped the heavy rubber on the ground.

He could have been real with Rachel the very first day she'd come to Mr. Farrell's door. But the lies. All those filthy lies! Now he had to undo the entire ugly mess.

A wrench slipped from Johnny's greasy fingers and clanked to the ground. His black-stained hands disgusted him. His dirty overalls stank from car lubricant.

As a customer drove in and waved him over, he looked up at the sign of his repair shop. His heart no longer sang at seeing his name up there. He wanted to tear it down and rip it to shreds.

Now he had to expose his true self to Rachel. He had to watch her face wrench in disgust when she found out he was just a car mechanic not a brilliant billionaire entrepreneur as he'd pretended.

As Johnny spoke to his customer, his jaw muscles ached with tension. He didn't want Mr. Farrell to come back. He didn't want to permanently return to his suffocating rent-controlled apartment. He didn't want his enchanting relationship with Rachel to end. But the drums of doom were pounding at his forehead.

As Rachel typed Zane's case-study data into the computer at her office, she excitedly told Kim, "He's *everything* I want in a man!"

Kim peeked over Rachel's shoulder at the green screen. "Will your research on Farrell tell me what makes him so sexy?" Kim asked.

"Only my body knows for sure," Rachel replied, breaking into a girlish smile.

"You don't have to answer this," her friend began, "but I'm dying to know, anyway. Did your sex case study bring you to orgasm?"

"Kim, the question is—when *didn't* he?" she admitted, her cheeks warming with embarrassment.

"Wow!" Kim exclaimed. "You've finally got it."

"Got what?"

"A healthy sex image."

"What do you mean?" Rachel asked, suddenly feeling uneasy.

"Rachel, don't get mad," Kim said. "I know how sensitive and private you are about your sex life. That's why I never mentioned it before. But Kent—after he split with you—well, he had a big mouth."

Rachel's fingers froze on the keyboard, and she whirled in her seat. "Kent told everybody why he wouldn't marry me?" she asked, horrified.

All her friends and acquaintances knew she was oversexed! Her stomach clenched into a tight ball. She didn't know whether to scream or cry.

"Rachel, I never believed Kent," Kim explained. "And I was right. I met up with an old high-school friend of mine who is Kent's most recent fiancée."

"Kent's getting married?" Rachel asked in a low voice. She didn't care whether or not Kent had a wife. But knowing he'd rejected her because of sex but had accepted another woman momentarily brought back her feelings of inadequacy.

"My friend is his *ex*-fiancée," Kim quickly added. "She told me that Kent left her waiting at the altar, too."

"Did she say why?" Rachel asked, desperately needing to know.

"He called her a nymphomaniac," Kim revealed. "He said no man could ever satisfy her. All she wanted was sex, sex and more sex."

Rachel couldn't believe her ears. "Did she think there was something sexually wrong with her?"

"Yes," Kim replied. "But when I told her what Kent said about you, she realized that *she's* normal and *he's* the one who's afraid he can't sexually satisfy a woman."

"I can't believe this," Rachel said, as if she was waking up from a bad dream. "All this time I've been torturing myself thinking I had a sex problem, when it was *him?*"

She impulsively banged her palm on her desk and rose from her chair. Her body felt lighter, her mind freer.

"There was never anything sexually wrong with me," she said. "I have normal yearnings, normal needs." Wasn't that what Zane was trying to tell her? But now she knew it for herself. Now she could return to his arms feeling totally liberated and aware of the solid truth that she was a healthy sexy woman.

Just then, her telephone rang, but she was so wrapped up in utter amazement about her exhilarating self-realization, Kim answered it for her.

"Sure, hold on," Kim said into the receiver. She covered the mouthpiece and whispered to Rachel, "I think it's your paramour."

Rachel quickly grabbed the phone. "Zane? Where are you? I can't wait to see you!"

"I'm in my office," Johnny replied from his grungy car shop, feeling angry heat rush to his face at what he had to do. *Tell her you're a fake right now!* he silently yelled at himself. But he didn't want to reveal the truth over the shop phone. He needed to be able to see her, to touch her. "Rachel, can I see you right away?"

"Sure," she replied with such enthusiasm, it made Johnny feel lower than a street curb. "When?"

"How about right now?" Johnny suggested. He couldn't wait another second longer. He had to get the nightmare over with. And he had to face his punishment.

"Oh, Zane, yes!" Rachel said, so ecstatic he'd called.

Suddenly, she remembered that tonight was Kim's daughter Stacy's birthday. "Oh, wait a minute," she added. "I can't stay for long. I've got to go to a friend's birthday party."

Kim looked up from the sex-study papers. "Invite him over," her friend whispered.

"Zane, my friend Kim wants to know if you'll come with me," she said in an exhilarated voice. She'd love to introduce him to her "family."

Johnny's first impulse was to say yes. He yearned to fully merge his life with Rachel's, but it could never be. After he told her about all of his lying, she'd shove him out of her life like an infectious disease.

"Thanks, but I've got to pass," Johnny managed to say. He felt as though the life energy was being drained out of him.

"I'll meet you at your house in a couple of hours," she told him.

As Johnny set down the greasy shop phone, he held his hand on the receiver for a moment longer as though it was his last call to her.

"Oh, I can't wait to be with him!" Rachel squealed like a teenager as she excitedly helped Kim put together the research package.

"Too bad Zane can't make Stacy's party tonight," Kim said. "I'm dying to meet him."

"Don't worry, you'll all get to know Zane," she said happily. "Maybe we'll invite the three of you over to dinner at his house in Bel Air."

"My, oh, my, aren't you the one with all the plans," Kim commented with a smile.

"I can't help it, Kim," Rachel said, dizzy with joy. "Zane's so perfect for me. I'm so elated I can barely think!"

As she picked up Zane's case-study printout, the papers slipped out of her hands and landed directly in the trash can. The accident momentarily jolted her.

"I hope that's not an omen," Rachel said in a light tone, but inside, she felt an uneasiness she couldn't quite explain.

In the university parking lot, Rachel turned the ignition key to start her Valiant, but the engine knocked and rolled over a few times. Not wanting to waste time to get it started, Rachel asked Kim to drop her off at Zane's house.

On the hilly, winding road up to his Bel Air estate in Kim's car, Rachel replayed Zane's phone conversation with her. Along with the joy, she'd sensed tension in his voice.

She kept telling herself not to worry. Yet, why couldn't she shake off the fear that Zane might be having last-minute doubts about her?

"What a spread!" Kim said as she drove through the opened King Kong gate of Zane's property. "What woman *wouldn't* fall for a single man with his wealth?"

"Zane means much much more to me than his fat wallet," Rachel told her friend.

"But you've got to admit that his mega money makes him more appealing, doesn't it?" Kim added with a laugh.

"Maybe," she said, not really sure that his multidollars made him more attractive to her.

As Rachel climbed out of Kim's car, her friend reminded her that she'd pick her up at six o'clock sharp.

Rachel nervously pressed the bell of the copper double doors. She desperately wanted her dream of being a couple with Zane to come true. But what if he was having second thoughts about whether she was right for him. What if—

No! she told herself finally. She wasn't going to let her old insecurities destroy her hopes and dreams with Zane. She'd finally found the perfect man, and she wasn't going to lose him.

She made a secret pact with herself. No matter what hesitations or doubts she heard in Zane's voice, she'd ignore them. She wanted Zane Farrell to be all hers, and she refused to let anything stand in her way.

As Johnny flew down the staircase, he promised himself, *Right off, you tell her who you really are. No more pretending. No more false fronts.*

But the moment Johnny yanked open the door, Rachel immediately went into his arms, and he was one with her again. He forgot he was in Bel Air. And he forgot about Mr. Farrell.

Johnny was only conscious of the intoxicating gardenia scent of her silken hair and her rosebud lips on his. As she tasted, licked and nibbled at him with abandon, he kicked the front door closed with his heel, desperately holding on to his last few moments with her.

As Johnny flew down the staircase he pressed himself
further back, waiting for ... a second to cross over him...
Johnny, no more than a child.

But the moment Johnny leaned over the rail, Rachel
touched the stage door, an ache deep in her heart. She
raised an imagined fist to ... ...

... to gaze only conscious of the loneliness. Johnny
stood in the ... and the ... opened, he to his ...
leash, barked and sniffed ... Tony, with affection he rubbed
the black door ... with his teeth despairingly, pushing
to his folder to smooth with his...

Eight

————

Rachel slid her fingers through Zane's curly hair and then
locked her hands at the back of his neck. She pressed her
clothed body against his, wanting to get closer to him, closer
than ever before.

Zane's lips nibbled at her earlobe, sending shivers along
her spine. She couldn't wait to merge her body with his
again. She quickly unbuttoned his shirt, pushed it aside and
spread her palms across his naked chest. She felt so free inside knowing she didn't have to restrain her sexuality anymore. She could respond to her impulses and give whatever
came naturally to her.

She put her face to his chest and slid her tongue across his
broad pectorals and licked his nipples.

She heard a low groan from deep within Zane's throat.
His strong hands yanked up her skirt in the back, and he slid
both palms inside the elastic waistband of her panties.

She gasped as he gripped the flesh of her buttocks and

pressed her pelvis into his fully expanded maleness. She knew he wanted her badly, just as badly as she desired him.

Zane grabbed the waistband of her panties and yanked them over her ankles. She felt the fresh air filter up her thighs to the aching area between her legs.

She realized they'd drifted near the sliding glass doors facing the turquoise kidney-shaped swimming pool.

Her mind flitted to an arousing fantasy, and she wasn't about to repress her deepest sexual desires a second longer.

"Zane," she whispered, out of breath.

Rachel's calling him Zane brought Johnny's mind back to stark reality.

He was in the living room of Mr. Farrell's mansion. And Rachel still thought he was Mr. Farrell.

"Rachel, I need to talk to you." Johnny forced the words out. His body was pulsating to link with hers. But he had to keep his mind on his goal.

He began to button up his shirt, needing to stay in control, knowing his flesh would weaken if she touched him again.

Rachel's fingers stopped Johnny from closing his shirt.

"Can't we talk later and go for a swim?" she suggested with a mischievous glint in her sensual brown eyes.

"Rachel, you don't understand," Johnny blurted out, feeling strangled by the truth wanting to come out. "I'm not the man you think I am."

"I know, I know," she said as she slipped his shirt off his broad shoulders and hurled it to the sofa. "You're a man who's frightened of commitment. You get too close and then you want to pull back. That's okay. I understand your feelings. I wouldn't change one single part of you."

"But I'm not—"

Rachel quickly shushed him up with her warm mouth over his.

Johnny couldn't think anymore. He was engulfed in the hotness of her lips and tongue. And he yearned for just a few more short minutes he had left with her.

Rachel took Zane's hand and pulled him onto the beaming sun-filled patio. She couldn't believe herself. She wasn't letting Zane finish what he wanted to say. Whatever doubts he had about himself or her, she didn't want to hear them. She'd show him he was everything she ever dreamed in a man and there was nothing for him to fear.

She uninhibitedly peeled off her dress under the steaming summer sun and dived naked into the turquoise-liquid pool. The cool water caressed every inch of her bare skin as she swam underwater for a few seconds and then surfaced, breathing in the fresh air.

She rubbed the water out of her eyes and pushed her dripping hair away so she could see again. She looked for Zane on the patio.

But he was gone.

"Zane?" she called out, momentarily wondering if she'd made a terrible mistake being so blatantly sexual with him.

Suddenly, she felt two powerful hands grip her waist from behind.

Zane whirled her around in his arms. His naked body glistened in the pool. His eyes were glazed. And he crushed her pulsating breasts to his bare wet chest. His eager mouth closed over hers.

Johnny's tongue slipped between Rachel's parted lips. He desperately needed to feel her body and soul close to him one final time. Just one last time naked and aroused with her. One last time of feeling her entire being wrapped as one with his. Then he'd be out of her life forever.

Johnny released his lips from hers and circled his hands around her swollen wet breasts. Her firm flesh trembled under his probing fingertips. He inserted each nipple in his mouth and suckled them.

Rachel groaned and arched her back, pushing her throbbing breasts deeper into his mouth. Johnny nibbled and bit the flesh of her globes until she wanted more.

She cried out in pleasure as he slipped his hand between her naked thighs and caressed the intimacy of her.

Johnny ached to be inside her. He couldn't wait any longer. He grabbed the condom he'd left by the side of the pool and slipped it on.

Then he clutched her bare buttocks and lifted her off the pool floor. When he spread her thighs apart, she automatically wrapped her legs around his waist.

Johnny pulled her against him and merged his body with hers. As he rhythmically moved inside her, her head flew back and she groaned. Powerful sensations flooded through his body, and his breaths came heavily in and out of his lungs.

Johnny peered deeply into Rachel's glassy eyes. He smiled at her. He wanted her to know that she was everything to him. That there was no woman alive as beautiful as her. And now he wished he could have her for always.

Her oval browns connected with Johnny's, and she smiled back as though she were in heaven, too. She squeezed her legs tighter around his waist as he delved deeper and deeper inside her, trying to reach the center of her soul. He felt her convulsing in orgasmic spasms at his every thrust.

"Rachel, Rachel," Johnny groaned from the core of his being as his body reached supreme arousal. Then he exploded inside the depths of her.

Johnny held her close against his body while his breathing gradually returned to normal. He kissed her cheeks, her forehead, the tip of her nose, her eyelids, her lips.

"I love you, Rachel, I love you," Johnny whispered over and over as he tenderly kissed her.

Her legs relaxed around his waist and slowly her feet settled onto the floor of the pool. She circled his waist with her arms and snuggled her face against his wet chest.

Johnny felt whole with her heart and soul entwined with his. There was nothing more he needed in life, nothing but her.

"I love you, too, Zane," she murmured back.

Hearing her call him Zane once again ricocheted Johnny back into fierce reality. He'd allowed himself a few ecstatic moments with her. Now his insides darkened with turmoil knowing what he must force himself to do.

"Rachel, I need to tell you something very important about myself," he began. "You've got to listen to me."

"Say anything," she cooed, kissing his chest. "I accept it all."

Johnny lifted her chin with his finger so he could look her directly in the eyes. The words banged against his brain like an uncontrolled metal hammer.

"Rachel, the truth is—"

The loud ringing of the doorbell cut into his next words.

"Oh, no, it's Kim!" Rachel blurted out. "I forgot about Stacy's birthday party. I've got to go." She released herself from Johnny's arms and scrambled out of the pool, grabbed her clothes and headed toward the pool house for a towel.

"But Rachel, you've got to listen!"

"Zane, I'm sorry," she hurriedly said. "I promise we'll talk tomorrow when I come over." Then she disappeared in the pool house.

Dammit! Dammit! Johnny slapped his fist into the turquoise water, sending a splash clear across the kidney-shaped pool. He was a coward not to have told her the second she'd walked through the front doors. But his powerful emotional and spiritual need for her had overshadowed his desire to tell her the truth about himself. He'd failed miserably.

Johnny angrily pulled himself out of the pool, and dripping with water, he slipped on his pants and shirt over his wet skin. Rachel came running out of the pool house fully dressed, with soaking strands of hair dangling across her beautiful face.

"I love you," she whispered happily as she kissed him on the lips. She was too much in a hurry, too elated, to notice his upset. "I'll see you tomorrow."

Then she was gone.

What the hell is wrong with me? Johnny silently screamed at himself. He clenched and unclenched his fists, unable to control the outrage. He was incensed at his own weakness to blurt out the truth to Rachel.

About to burst, Johnny furiously dived back into the pool, pants and all. He swam forceful laps back and forth, hoping that every ounce of his fury would dissolve into the depths of the water.

"Happy birthday to yooouuu! Happy birthday to yooouuu! You belong in the zooo!" sang Rachel to Stacy, totally out of harmony with Kim and her husband, Charlie.

Stacy giggled and excitedly clapped her hands at Rachel for singing her favorite part. Then she blew out her four candles—including one for good luck, of course—and Rachel cheered.

She helped Stacy dig out a gigantic piece of chocolate-chocolate-chip birthday cake and added two overflowing scoops of vanilla ice cream on top.

At that moment, Rachel truly felt like a second mother to Stacy. Yes, she had to admit it. She wanted a houseful of laughing little ones of her own—with Zane. Of course, she didn't know if he wanted children, but she had a sense he'd want a family as much as she did.

What was she thinking? He hadn't even asked her to marry him! She inwardly smiled, somehow knowing that it was going to happen. And when he did propose, she was sure he'd plan an elaborate wedding ceremony and reception at the wealthiest, trendiest ballroom in Los Angeles.

And this time, she didn't have to worry about him not showing up at the altar.

As Stacy giggled opening her birthday presents, Rachel sat on the floor to help her tear off the wrapping paper. She wondered whether she really wanted an ultra-expensive wedding reception. Actually, she felt more comfortable with the idea of simplicity and frugality. That's the life she was used to. Although, maybe she *could* adjust to his upper-crust formal-dinner-party life-style if she tried.

"Time for bed, birthday girl," Kim announced to Stacy as she cleaned up the birthday mess.

"I want Aunt Rachel to put me to bed!" Stacy insisted.

"If it's okay with your mommy, it's okay with me," Rachel agreed.

Kim nodded and then Rachel lifted cute Stacy into her arms and went to get her bath ready. By the time she had Stacy under the sheets and had read her Dr. Seuss, the little girl was fast asleep.

Feeling as content as a cat taking a nap in the sun, Rachel returned to the living room to find Kim and Charlie talking about the steel company where he was a top executive.

"I wish the company had picked *me* for that big business conference in Paris," Charlie said to his wife as Rachel entered the room. "Every entrepreneur in the world attended that affair. Just think, Kim, I could've taken you to romantic Parie while Rachel baby-sat Stacy."

"Mmm, sounds *so* delicious," Kim said, cuddling up to her husband on the sofa.

"You're both such romantics," Rachel said. "I love it!"

This time, she didn't feel an ounce of envy at the solid relationship Kim had with Charlie. She flashed on her and Zane in his Bel Air swimming pool engulfed in each other's naked bodies. And the love—oh, the blissful love they'd expressed to each other. No, she wasn't envious at all. Now she had a deep love relationship of her own.

Rachel sat on the lounge chair and took a sip from the cup of cappuccino that Charlie had made for her.

"Kim tells me you're one happy woman these days," Charlie commented as he got up and poured another cup of cappuccino for his wife.

"I'm completely, totally, all-encompassingly euphoric," Rachel admitted, leaning back in utter relaxation.

"Who's the lucky guy?" Charlie inquired. He sat down close to Kim and slipped his arm around her shoulders.

"I already told you his name, Charlie," Kim said. "See, your mind is on business so much these days, you don't even listen to me."

"Okay, I admit, I've got stuffed ears sometimes," he said, nipping her earlobe with his teeth.

"I'm serious, Charlie!" Kim said as she started to laugh.

"The man I'm hooked on is Zane Farrell," Rachel said, smiling at the two love doves.

Charlie stopped nibbling and stared at Rachel. "*The* Zane Farrell?" he asked a bit hesitantly.

It was the way he said it that immediately put Rachel on guard.

"Why, yes," she said. "Do you know him?"

"He's on the board of directors of our company," Charlie replied. "I saw his name was on the list of entrepreneurs attending a Paris conference last week."

Charlie abruptly got off the sofa and refilled their cappuccino cups.

"Zane didn't go to Paris last week," Rachel said, feeling that same uneasiness she'd felt before. "In fact, he never mentioned the Paris conference at all."

Rachel felt Charlie deliberately avoiding her as he turned on the television set. She felt her muscles tense as she sensed that he knew something about Zane that he didn't want to tell her.

"Charlie, what's wrong?" Kim asked, noticing the change in him, too.

"Nothing," he replied in a low voice. He flipped the remote, switching from station to station with no apparent goal in mind, except to avoid the issue of Zane Farrell.

"What do you know about Zane?" Rachel managed to say.

Charlie remained silent, still switching the remote.

"Charlie," Kim insisted. "If it's something Rachel should know, wouldn't it be unfair not to tell her?"

"It's only a stupid rumor," Charlie finally replied. "I hate rumors."

"I don't care," Rachel pursued, sitting on the edge of the chair, knowing something was wrong, very wrong. "I want to know, Charlie."

Charlie's jaw muscles tensed. "I don't like this one bit." He stopped for a second. "The execs at my company said that Zane Farrell was going to Paris because that's where his French girlfriend lives."

Rachel's throat felt tight and dry. She got up from the chair and brought her cup into the kitchen so she could be alone. French girlfriend? Her thoughts raced back to when she was making love with Zane in his Bel Air pool. He'd wanted to tell her something important. Was it about his other life in Paris? But she wouldn't listen to him.

Oh, God, she couldn't take it. She didn't know what to believe about him anymore!

Kim and Charlie came into the kitchen.

"Charlie, tell Rachel the rumor is meaningless," Kim insisted, clearly worried about her friend.

"Kim's right," Charlie agreed. "Sure, maybe Farrell had a girlfriend in Paris at one time, but now he has you."

"You see!" Kim said quickly. "That's why Zane didn't go to Paris for the conference or this other woman. He fell in love with you, Rachel."

"Thanks, guys," she said with all the strength she could muster. "It's late, and I'd better be getting home." Her head felt as heavy as concrete. She clasped her trembling hands together. "Stacy's birthday party was great. Thanks for inviting me."

Charlie glanced helplessly at Kim as Rachel tried to make it to the front door without showing how devastatingly raw with pain she felt inside.

Kim shooed Charlie away as if he'd done enough damage for the evening, and followed Rachel outside to drive her home.

"Rachel, you love him," Kim said as she drove, "and he loves you."

"Doesn't love mean being honest?" she asked, trying to stop the blurry tears from coming.

"Yes, of course, but—"

"Kim, I need time to think," was all Rachel could say. She promised herself that she wasn't going to cry until she got to her apartment. She wasn't going to think about how perfect she wanted everything to be between her and Zane.

When Kim dropped her off, she hugged her friend for caring and then rushed out of the car before Kim noticed the tears burning her eyes.

Under the starlit evening sky, Johnny struggled to focus on watering his tomato plants at his Santa Monica rent-controlled apartment. Ways to tell Rachel the truth about himself raked through his brain like a sharp-edged razor.

No matter how much he tried to sugarcoat his dreaded conversation with her, Johnny knew he'd have to admit to being an uneducated, dirty car repairman.

Dammit! Dammit! Dammit! He angrily turned off the water and threw the hose onto the ground. The vegetable garden he tended and nurtured suddenly seemed pedestrian. Everything about his entire existence felt mediocre and insignificant.

He should have never accepted Mr. Farrell's house-sitting offer. Being Mr. Farrell was a crazy nonsensical idea. And he should have never fallen deeply, crazily in love with Professor Rachel Smith.

Johnny prepared for a long, sleepless night in his apartment. He kept the lamplight on and sat at the small round table in his kitchen. He suddenly hated his cramped apartment. He wanted to break free of being Johnny Wells and be somebody great like Zane Farrell so Rachel would keep loving him.

The moment Rachel entered her apartment, a rush of tears filled her eyes. In a blur, she quickly picked up the phone to dial Zane's number. She pressed the buttons of the first three digits and then hung up.

She was in no state to talk to him. She took off her clothes and climbed into the shower. She leaned her head back and let the cool water spread over her hair and face. Salty tears mingled and coursed to her lips. Zane was her man. He'd accepted the side of herself that she had despised.

She couldn't give him up that easily.

She forcefully turned off the faucet and grabbed her towel. She used hard strokes to dry her body, determined to find out the truth about Zane Farrell's secret life.

No more hiding parts of himself from her. She would search for the jugular vein of honesty within him. And she would find it.

The next morning, Johnny hurriedly left the work at his repair shop to Tito and raced his pickup up the private road to Mr. Farrell's mansion in Bel Air knowing D day had arrived.

Rachel would be over in an hour.

This time, Johnny parked his truck in front of the mansion instead of hiding it in Mr. Farrell's garage. He didn't shed his greasy coveralls and oil-stained shirt. He didn't try to scrub the grime from under his fingernails. He didn't put on wrinkle-free pants to look Mr. Farrell-suitable.

Johnny planned to stay Johnny Wells inside and out.

In the spacious living room, he paced the floor. He nervously glanced at his watch. Thirty more minutes and Rachel would be standing in front of him.

No more game playing. No more avoiding the words that would inevitably shatter the intimate relationship he'd developed with her.

He wouldn't let himself weaken when he saw her beautiful brown eyes peering lovingly into his. He wouldn't look at her rosebud lips waiting to be kissed. He wouldn't dare allow himself to caress her soft sensual body. That would end his resolve right there.

With his greasy hand, he wiped away the beads of perspiration forming on his forehead. He shoved both hands into his coverall pockets. He took a long deep breath of control.

I'm ready, he told himself.

Just then, the sound of the doorbell echoed through the mansion. For a second, Johnny's limbs froze. Rachel was twenty-five minutes early. He knew he wasn't ready. He'd never be ready to end it with the woman he loved more than his own life.

As he moved toward the front door to destroy his once-happy fate, his leather work boots felt heavy, as if they were made of solid steel.

His gut ached as he yanked open the copper doors to greet Rachel for the last time.

"Rachel, I—" His voice caught in his throat.

George, Mr. Farrell's chauffeur, was standing there. Behind him was a shiny black stretch limousine parked in back of Johnny's pickup truck. The black-tinted windows were closed to shield the contents of the interior.

George politely cleared his throat. "Johnny, Mr. Farrell asks for your forgiveness," George began, "but he has arrived a trifle earlier than expected."

Johnny's eyes widened in utter horror. "Mr. Farrell's here *now?* But he can't—" His gaze shot to the black stretch wishing it would go away.

"I am sorry for the intrusion," George went on. "Mr. Farrell's new French wife has also accompanied him."

"Mr. Farrell got married?" Johnny asked. "Why, that's great! I guess he wants me out of his house pronto, right?"

"Mr. Farrell apologizes profusely for his abrupt return," George said. "As soon as you get back to your car shop, he will phone you for an update on his affairs."

"Yeah, sure, of course," Johnny told the chauffeur.

He struggled to remain levelheaded, but frantic thoughts of Rachel's arriving at the mansion ricocheted back and forth in the depths of his skull.

As Johnny headed for his pickup, he courteously waved to Mr. Farrell behind the concealed windows of the limo. One black-tinted pane slid down a few inches, and Mr. Farrell's hand appeared and waved back at him.

Johnny peeled his truck off Mr. Farrell's property. He could barely contain himself. His greasy hands gripped the steering wheel so hard he thought he'd crack it in half.

As he drove down the curvy roads of Bel Air, he kept frantically looking for Rachel's green car, even though it was too early for her to come.

What the hell was he going to do? First, he had to rush back to the shop to receive Mr. Farrell's phone call. But what about Rachel? She was on her way to see him at Mr. Farrell's house. But he wouldn't be there to greet her. The real Mr. Farrell would!

An emotional pain ripped through Johnny's body, as though his limbs were being torn from opposite ends.

"Man, oh, man, oh, man!" he yelled. "What the hell am I going to do?"

Nine

Johnny screeched his truck to a short stop at the shop. He checked his watch. Ten more minutes and Rachel was scheduled to arrive at Mr. Farrell's house. If she was consistent, she'd be ten to fifteen minutes late, the way she always was. Or better yet, she might be delayed at the university.

Johnny prayed for the last option.

As he rushed to his small office past waiting customers, Tito was on the phone waving to Johnny and saying into the receiver, "Yes, Mr. Farrell, Johnny has just arrived."

Tito quickly handed Johnny the phone.

"Mr. Farrell," Johnny began, out of breath, not knowing what to say because all he could think about was Rachel on her way to Farrell's house.

"Johnny, I truly apologize for returning home without giving you ample warning," Mr. Farrell said. "I am sure George informed you that I have finally taken wedding vows with my beautiful French lady."

"Yes, congratulations, Mr. Farrell," Johnny told him. He was happy for Mr. Farrell because he wouldn't be lonely anymore.

"Johnny, is something wrong?"

"Mr. Farrell, I need your help," he blurted out, feeling as if his chest would cave in if he didn't tell Mr. Farrell. "I'm in a major bind."

"Johnny, what can I do?" Mr. Farrell asked.

"I'm in love with Professor Rachel Smith from the university sex study," he said in a rush of syllables. "But she thinks I'm you. And this morning I was going to tell her the truth at your house. But now you're home and—"

"Do not worry, Johnny," Mr. Farrell said. "I shall handle the matter. I will explain the entire misunderstanding to her when she arrives."

"No, Mr. Farrell," Johnny said firmly. "I appreciate your suggestion, but I need to tell her myself. You understand, don't you, Mr. Farrell? It's got to be me."

"Of course, Johnny."

Johnny frantically looked at his watch. Five more minutes, if she was on time.

"Can you keep the front gates of your property closed, Mr. Farrell?" Johnny asked. "I'll try to catch up with her there."

"Sure, Johnny, sure," Mr. Farrell told him.

"Thanks," Johnny said, knowing that the man had always been there for him.

When Johnny hung up, he quickly dialed Rachel's office number, hoping she'd been delayed. But her answering machine picked up his call. He banged down the receiver in frustration without leaving a message. Then he scrambled out of the office.

Several customers were impatiently waiting for Johnny's assistance, and he hated leaving them with only Tito there, but he had to catch Rachel at Mr. Farrell's front gate.

* * *

The deejay on the car radio in Rachel's Valiant announced the time before he put an old Beatles song on the air.

Why can't you ever be on time? Rachel scolded herself.

She pressed her foot farther down on the gas pedal, but instead of speeding up, her Valiant sputtered and slowed.

"Come on!" she yelled at her car. She was already fifteen minutes late. She was still on Sunset Boulevard and hadn't even reached the winding roads of Bel Air.

All because of her stupid car. She'd had trouble getting it started again. It had stalled out on her twice since she hit Sunset Boulevard and caused honking car horns to bellow until she got it started again.

She wished she could helicopter her way straight to the front door of Zane's house. She had to find out the truth about Zane's other life. She was going to listen to him this time. She prayed that whatever he revealed wouldn't threaten the love growing between them.

Suddenly, a loud clanking came from her engine. She tensed up in the seat as her car huffed and puffed along Sunset Boulevard. Her eyes widened in horror as steam seeped out from under the hood.

Her gaze darted to the temperature gauge. The arrow had entered the dangerous overheating zone!

She knew her car would never make it up the hilly, curvy roads of Bel Air. She had to call Zane and ask him to pick her up.

She made a right turn off Sunset Boulevard onto a side street, searching for a place to park so she could find a public phone. But she was on a residential street lined with expensive houses.

She wanted to scream out in frustration. But she continued driving, constantly glancing at the temperature gauge as it hovered at very hot. The thick white engine steam blew into the windshield, making it difficult to see anything in front of her.

Through the white smoke, she finally spotted a service station up ahead. She nervously directed her car into the parking lot, praying she wouldn't hit anything or anyone on the way. Through the misty haze, she saw the sign above the shop which read Johnny's Foreign Automotive Repairs.

Johnny paced in front of Mr. Farrell's property gate with his eyes pinned on the road. He'd been staring so hard searching for Rachel's car that his vision was blurring.

Johnny anxiously kicked the tip of his work boots on the gravel ground. Why was this happening to him? Why couldn't he have a trickle of Mr. Farrell's luck and have a woman like Rachel love him for who he was? He knew he never would've met Rachel if it hadn't been for Mr. Farrell's prestigious life-style. A woman like her needed a man who was hooked up to superior intelligence and power.

Not to you, Johnny Wells, he painfully reminded himself. *Not to you.*

His ears perked up as the grinding of an engine approached. But the car zipped on down the road. Was he relieved that it wasn't her? Maybe he was. Maybe part of him was still hoping he could keep the illusion of Mr. Farrell so he'd still have Rachel as his love.

He looked at his watch. Remembering the waiting customers he'd left behind at the shop, he knew he couldn't afford to lose any business. He was on the verge of destroying his relationship with Rachel, but he couldn't allow his business to go under, too.

He decided to wait at the gate a few more minutes, and if Rachel didn't show, he'd alert Mr. Farrell and be forced to return to his shop.

The white steam blew into Rachel's face as she stood helplessly near her Valiant's engine. She felt torn between tending to her sick car and calling Zane, who was probably worrying about her whereabouts.

She headed toward the repair shop. She couldn't believe all the people lined up waiting for assistance. And there was only one South American auto mechanic out there to help.

"Excuse me!" Rachel yelled, squeezing in between the other customers. "Could you look at my car? I'm really worried it might blow!"

"Ma'am, you must wait your turn," the South American man told her apologetically. "You see the problem I am having with so many other customers." He glanced outside at the steam pouring out of her car. "Looks like you have a radiator problem. I will be with you shortly." Then he returned to a businessman in a suit who was explaining his car troubles, while a young mother with two kids looked worriedly at her own old car.

"But sir, it'll take just a second of your time," Rachel insisted as the other customers gave her the deadly eye.

"Please, ma'am, you must be patient," he insisted.

"Isn't there anyone else who can help me?"

"I am sorry, ma'am, but I am the sole mechanic available," the man explained.

"Where's the owner?" she asked, frustrated. "I want to talk to the owner of this place."

"He momentarily left," the South American told her with troubled eyes. "But he will be right back."

"But my car!" she exclaimed, feeling exasperated as she stared at the thick steam emanating from her car like smoke from a ferocious fire.

Frantically remembering Zane, she quickly turned back to the mechanic.

"Can I use your telephone?" she begged. "It's really important."

"Sure," he replied. "Back there in the office."

"Thanks," she said, hurrying into the tiny space he called an office.

The room was as greasy and oily as the workshop. But as Rachel maneuvered her body so she wouldn't hit her clean clothes against the blackened wooden desk and creaky chair, she felt a sudden warmth being in that room.

There were green plants with lush leaves overflowing on the windowsill. There was a book on plant life lying on the cluttered desk and another book on nurturing a vegetable garden. For a second, she couldn't help smiling at the man who inhabited this cramped office. Car engines and gardening? He was quite a character, she decided.

She finally located the telephone under a pile of papers. Before she had a chance to dial Zane's number, her eye caught the owner's name printed at the bottom of a Johnny's Foreign Automotive Repairs bill. She stopped for a moment. There was something familiar about the name. She slowly set down the phone.

"Johnny Wells," she whispered. Where had she heard that name?

Then it hit her. She remembered the telephone call at Zane's house. The man on the phone from Cairo had asked to speak to Johnny Wells. But didn't Zane say that Johnny Wells was his full-time chauffeur?

Why would his chauffeur's name be printed on the repair-shop bill as the owner? It had to be a different Johnny Wells.

Rachel put the bill back on the desk, feeling a thicker cloud of doubt filling her mind. Was this another fact Zane had neglected to tell her? But why?

She felt an aching pain rise within her. Why didn't Zane want to have a completely open and honest relationship with her? Didn't he realize that was the only kind of intimacy she could ever accept with him?

She was about to pick up the receiver to dial Zane's number, when the shop phone rang. The South American man hurried into the office, excused himself to her and answered the call.

* * *

Johnny frantically raced his pickup back down the curvy Bel Air road to return to his shop. He couldn't wait for Rachel a moment longer.

He had buzzed Mr. Farrell at the locked gate and asked if George could answer the buzzer when Rachel arrived and for the chauffeur to tell her that he'd be back in a little while and then call him at the shop to come over.

Mr. Farrell had said he'd be glad to and apologized again for his unannounced return and the trouble he'd caused Johnny.

Johnny screeched his pickup to a stop in the small lot of his repair shop. He jumped out, and from the corner of his eye, he noticed steam rushing out of a car engine in the lot.

His lungs froze. It couldn't be! Rachel's car was sitting in his lot. And it was in severe need of repair.

"Rachel?" Johnny called as he ran toward her car. "Rachel!" He hoped nothing had happened to her. He prayed that she hadn't been in an accident. His mind was so crazy with worry about her that he totally forgot about his Mr. Farrell dilemma. But she wasn't near the car.

He yanked a greasy rag out of his coveralls and lifted the hot engine hood to let out the steam. He stepped back as the white vapor blew out from the overheated radiator.

Johnny hurried into his crowded workshop looking for Rachel, but he was blocked by impatient customers complaining about their car troubles.

Inside the shop office, Rachel nervously waited for the South American man to get off the phone so she could call Zane.

The moment he did, she took the receiver and started dialing, when she heard the mechanic tell her, "Ma'am, here comes the owner."

Just then, Zane barged into the office. "Tito, that overheated Valiant outside—"

Rachel's mind was spinning as she took in Zane's greasy coveralls and his black-stained hands.

"The overheated job belongs to this lady," Tito said as he hurried back to the waiting customers.

"*You* own this shop?" Rachel forced out, feeling a rise of fury envelope her, realizing he'd concealed *another* area of his life!

"Rachel, I want to explain—" Zane began, reaching out to touch her arm.

She pulled back. "Why didn't you tell me that you had a repair shop?"

"Because I—"

At that moment, Tito hurried back into the office. "A lady's brakes are not working," Tito said to Zane. "She has two little children with her. It is a dangerous situation. You must come right now."

Tito was already out the door, obviously expecting Zane to follow.

"Rachel, will you wait for me right here?" he begged. "I'll tell you everything. I promise."

"Sure," she said, but the word came out cold and distant.

She leaned against his desk, trembling. Her hand rested on the repair bill she'd seen before. She picked up the invoice and stared at the name Johnny Wells, feeling so confused she couldn't think anymore.

Just then, Tito dashed into the office to grab a car key hanging on a nail on the wall.

Before he left, she called out, "Wait!" She desperately needed to get some answers.

"Yes, ma'am?"

"Who is Johnny Wells?"

"My boss," he replied. "The man that was just in here." She couldn't be hearing right!

"But—but I thought I heard someone call him Zane Farrell," she stammered.

"Oh, no, no, ma'am," Tito said, suddenly smiling. "What you heard is not true. Johnny only pretended to be Mr. Farrell. He was taking care of Mr. Farrell's house in Bel Air while Mr. Farrell was on a world tour."

"He was *house-sitting?*" she said tightly, suddenly feeling as if she was gasping for air.

"No more," Tito went on. "Mr. Farrell is back from Paris."

"I—I see," she croaked. Her brain was racing. The Paris conference Charlie had talked about. Zane Farrell's French girlfriend. Mrs. Guillino calling Zane her car mechanic. All the ugly pieces were fitting into place.

"Johnny sure did a successful job of convincing people he was Mr. Farrell," Tito commented just before he left. "Why, he was so good, he even fooled a smart professor from the university."

Johnny frantically checked the worn brakes of the car on the hydraulic lift belonging to the lady with the kids. Then he waved Tito over.

"Change these front and back pads right away," he ordered, even though he had customers waiting before her. "I don't want her and her kids leaving here with her brakes half-functioning."

"Sure thing, Johnny," Tito replied.

Johnny turned to his other customers. "I'm really sorry for the delay," he told them. "I'll be right with you. I'll be glad to take off ten percent from your bill for the inconvenience—"

Suddenly, Rachel stormed out of his office. Her usual warm brown eyes were ice picks digging into his soul as she walked past him as if he didn't even exist.

"Rachel, wait!" he called out, realizing she knew it all and watching his world shatter before his very eyes. He excused himself to his customers and rushed out of the shop.

Rachel rushed to her car, but Johnny ran after her, grabbed her shoulder and whirled her around.

"Don't go, please," Johnny begged.

She yanked his hand off as though he had a fatal infectious disease, the very same hand that such a short while ago had set fire to her naked body.

"You're a liar, *Johnny Wells!*" she shouted, angry blood rushing to her face.

"Rachel, let me explain—"

"Why?" she sharply cut in. "So you can tell me more Zane Farrell stories?"

"I had a reason for—"

"I don't care, Zane, Johnny, whoever you are!" she blurted. "I trusted you!" Her voice caught, and she looked away.

Impulsively, Johnny reached out, wanting to hold her, but knowing she despised him, his hand fell back to his side.

"Rachel, I know I deceived you," Johnny began, his heart ripping in two as he saw the torture in her eyes. "I wanted to tell you the truth so many times."

"How could you let me believe you were a brilliant, wealthy entrepreneur, when all the time you were just a—a car mechanic!"

Rachel's words seared through straight to his soul. His body felt numb. He couldn't speak. He clenched his fists until the knuckles were bloodred.

"I don't blame you for hating me," he managed to say. "You're right. I'm a fake. I don't own a big mansion or a red Porsche. I don't even have a high-school diploma."

"Why should I believe anything you say?" she retorted. "You don't know how to speak the truth. If you did, you would have never let me go on lov—" Her voice cracked.

She slammed down the hood of her car and jumped into the front seat. She struggled to start the engine, but it kept rolling over. She turned the ignition key again and again and again, but her car wouldn't start.

Johnny wasn't thinking as he went to the front of her car to lift up the hood to check the engine.

Rachel leaned out her window and shouted, "Get away from my car!"

"But I can fix it right now," Johnny began. "I can—"

"No! Stay away from me!" she cried out. "Just stay away!"

Stunned, Johnny slowly backed away from her vehicle. As she climbed out, he could see tears forming in her eyes. With a shaky hand, she locked her door.

Without looking at him, as though he wasn't even worth eyeing, she said, "I'll find a way to get my car out of your shop."

"Rachel, you can leave it here for as long as—"

"I'll have it towed out of here by the end of the day," she cut in coldly, ignoring him.

Then Rachel exploded out of the parking lot of Johnny's Foreign Automotive Repairs.

Rachel thought she heard Zane, Johnny, whoever, calling after her one last time. But she didn't turn around. She started running faster and faster to get away, far, far away from him.

Her heart was burning with fiery pain. Her lungs were so constricted she could barely take a breath.

Suddenly, sobs tore at her body. She didn't care who stared at her on the street. She didn't care at all about anything anymore.

She had no idea where she was running. Finally, through a blur of tears, she reached a pay phone and called a cab to take her back to the university.

As Rachel waited on the sidewalk for the taxi, she searched through her briefcase for a tissue. She suddenly found the pink button that had come off her blouse that day at the L.A. Art Museum. She squeezed it in her palm, remembering how close she'd felt to him that day on the shaded path. And how, through all her doubts and fears, she'd finally shared her flesh and spirit with him in passionate lovemaking at the Mexican cabana. The cabana she thought belonged to him.

Trembling with fury, she hurled the pink button into the asphalt street. At that moment, the huge wheels of a trailer truck ran over her button, as if her heart was being trampled. And when the truck was gone, the plastic lay in the street filthy and defiled. The way she felt inside.

Because Johnny Wells had used her.

She'd gone to Zane Farrell's house to do the sex interview, and Johnny Wells had deliberately taken advantage of the situation. He'd seen how turned on she was by him. He'd played along with her, letting her trust him until all her steel defenses had melted away.

And she'd fallen for his act. She'd opened her heart to him—and her legs.

She covered her face with both hands, feeling humiliated and shamed by her actions. She had been unable to resist his arousing touch. She'd forgotten the university study she'd been assigned and had succumbed to her bodily sensations and the flutter of her heart thinking he loved her.

Pedestrians passed her on the sidewalk, but she didn't dare look any of them in the eye. She was ashamed of herself for being so overpowered by sex that she didn't recognize the glaring warnings in front of her.

And there had been many signs blatantly screaming at her that Zane Farrell was not Zane Farrell.

Her cab arrived. She sat low in the worn back seat, not wanting the driver to see her tortured face. Why hadn't she yielded to the first message that could have alerted her to the truth?

On her initial phone call asking him for an appointment for the sex study interview, he hadn't even known what she was talking about. But she was so excited, so filled with neophyte enthusiasm about her first research project that she'd let it pass her by.

Then, upon meeting him face-to-face at Zane Farrell's mansion, she'd sensed that he didn't fit into that wealthy-echelon upper-class life-style. Yet, she was so attracted to him, she'd let her hormones take over. And she'd lost all semblance of analytical thought.

Rachel paid the taxi driver and rushed into her university office, not wanting to see or talk to anyone.

She was relieved that her office was empty. But as she closed her door to block out the rest of the world, Kim pushed through, carrying a stack of papers in both hands.

When Kim saw Rachel's face, she immediately dropped the stack onto her desk with a very worried look.

"What happened?" Kim asked.

"I—I'll be okay," Rachel stammered, telling herself that she was fine now. She was clear on the issues, and there was nothing to talk about.

"Tell me," her friend pursued.

Rachel stared down at the pencils on her desk that needed sharpening. Her throat felt tight. She shook her head, unable to speak. She wasn't going to allow any more tears. She wasn't!

"What happened with Zane?" Kim persisted.

"Zane?" Rachel repeated with sudden cold sarcasm. "The man I interviewed was not Zane Farrell."

"What are you talking about?"

"While Zane Farrell was in Cairo and Paris, I interviewed his *house-sitter,* Johnny Wells," she said. "He owns a repair shop and fixes cars! Can you believe it? And I thought he was the man of my dreams."

Rachel sucked in her breath and quickly brushed at the tears forming again in her eyes. She rushed on to tell her about how Johnny Wells had pretended to be Zane Farrell for her benefit.

"Oh, Rachel," Kim whispered, gently touching her friend's arm. "I'm sorry."

"What a mountain of laughs he had," she went on. "Here's this stupid professor thinking she's interviewing the real Zane Farrell about his sex life. And to top it off, she freely offers her naked body to him as a surprise bonus to the study! Boy, he made out good, didn't he?"

"Rachel, don't do this to yourself," Kim begged.

"Why? I'm an easy make, right? Just call Professor Rachel Smith for a sex interview, and she'll throw in her body, too!"

Rachel covered her ashamed face with her hands. What had she done? How could she have disgraced herself so?

She felt Kim soothingly rubbing her back. "Rachel, you made a mistake. The same thing could have happened to me."

"No, Kim," Rachel insisted. "You wouldn't have lowered yourself the way I did."

"Rachel, stop!"

But she couldn't hold back. "The university study would have remained your priority, Kim. But I let myself drown in sexual reverie with him, and I forgot my job. I ruined the university project with a fraudulent paper."

"Don't worry about the study," Kim told her. "I'll remove his papers from the research file and destroy them myself. Nobody will ever know."

"But I loved him, Kim, I loved him." She stared out her office window at the students walking on the path.

What tormented her the most—what she couldn't tell Kim—was that she'd found a love that accepted the part of herself she'd hated the most. But that love had never existed. Johnny Wells had played one hilarious joke on her.

The heavy metal wrench slipped out of Johnny's unsteady fingers and clanked to the blackened workshop floor. When he reached down to pick it up, his arm knocked over an open can of oil on the table, spilling it all over his work boots.

"Dammit!" he yelled out, frustrated.

"Johnny, you are no good at working today," Tito said. "Go home. I will take care of the shop. You will feel better in the morning."

"No, Tito," Johnny said, angrily soaking up the oil with a rag. "Tomorrow's not going to help. And neither is next week."

Ever since Rachel had stormed out of the shop, his heart had crumbled into tiny pieces. And his mind no longer wanted to function.

But Johnny knew he couldn't let his emotions interfere with his work. He had to keep his business going, not just for him, but Tito's job was at stake, too.

"I am sorry, Johnny," Tito went on. "I did not know it was her. It is all my fault. If I did not tell the professor—"

"Tito, it's *my* fault, not yours," Johnny reassured him. "I'm the one who lied to her."

Johnny dug the wrench into a customer's car engine trying to block out the suffering he'd caused Rachel and himself.

"You are not a terrible man, Johnny," Tito said.

"Sure, Tito, sure," he said, unable to believe Tito's words as the agonizing ache on Rachel's horrified face flashed through his mind.

"Johnny, you followed Mr. Farrell's orders," Tito said with sympathetic eyes. "You must not keep punching yourself."

Johnny stopped working on the engine. "I had no right to get emotionally involved with her. That wasn't part of my deal with Mr. Farrell. And I kept the deceitful act going, Tito. I didn't have the guts to tell her the truth."

"Because you love her, Johnny," Tito said. "Sometimes even a good man will lie to keep the woman he loves."

Johnny stared at Tito, desperately wanting to believe him but finding it so very, very hard.

Just then, a lumberjack-looking guy in a plaid shirt walked into the shop. "Can you sign this sheet, buddy?" the man asked Johnny. "I need to get the green car off your lot."

Johnny's eyes darted to Rachel's Valiant, which was already chained up to the tow truck.

Panic lightninged through Johnny's muscles. He turned back to the tow-truck driver. "But I repaired her car. I put in a new radiator and exhaust system. I can drive it to her myself."

"The lady gave me clear instructions to haul it outta here," the driver flatly said. "I'm just doin' my job, buddy."

The guy handed Johnny a pen for his signature. Johnny's fingers tightened around it. He stared at Rachel's Valiant, not wanting to release her car from his shop. As if the car was a part of her that was still in his life, and he couldn't let it go.

"I ain't got a decade," the man impatiently prompted.

"Yeah, sure," Johnny quickly said and then signed the piece of paper.

Johnny stood with his hands deep in his pockets watching the tow truck pull Rachel's green Valiant out of his lot.

His eyes strained to catch the last few seconds of her car going down the road, as though it were a vital limb of his being torn out of his body.

As Rachel's car finally disappeared off the street, Johnny clenched his teeth so tightly that a cramp pierced across his jaw. But the physical pain wasn't nearly as acute as the wrenching emotion exploding in his heart, knowing that Rachel Smith was out of his life forever.

Ten

As Chester Zole examined his last patient in the examining room, Rachel waited in his office. Chester had invited her over because he was excited about showing her something.

Rachel stared at the life-size model of the human skeleton standing in the corner. The skull and bones looked as cold and barren as she felt inside. Several weeks had passed of not seeing the man who'd been Zane. She'd tried to keep busy revising the sexuality research at her office.

Eliminating Zane Farrell's case study had been like slicing out one of her lungs. She'd tried to remain detached as she deleted all his sexual responses from the research by telling herself that Zane wasn't Zane. Therefore, the man she'd fallen in love with had never existed at all.

But then she read his answer about what part of a woman's body turned him on the most. And she remembered the way he'd said, "Your—I mean, a woman's breasts." And she flashed on the way his sea-blue eyes had yearned to caress her and how she'd ached for him to do so. How could she forget the electric currents that had sparked between them? Or how her heart had invited him in.

But her spirit shrank as she remembered the oil-stained red shirt she'd worn over her naked body, the shirt which she thought belonged to Zane. The shirt that was really Johnny Wells's.

She flashed on an image of Johnny Wells sitting in Zane Farrell's living room silently gloating that she was totally nude under his shirt. Smiling to himself when she gullibly believed his expressions of love in the Mexican cabana. Johnny Wells who inwardly chuckled that she'd abandoned her research and professionalism to make unabashed, uninhibited love to him.

Rachel turned away from the skeleton in Chester's office cringing at her abhorrent actions. She wanted to hate the fake Zane Farrell for cruelly tricking her. She wanted to strike out at him for humiliating her. But she couldn't. There was still a place in her heart that wished Zane could be Zane again. And that the love they had shared could still flourish and never, ever die.

She stared out the window at the L.A. palm trees, wanting to scream at herself for still being the stupid fool. Because deep down, she couldn't believe that Zane was gone. She didn't know if she'd ever be able to accept that he never really existed.

"Rachel, your posture needs improving," Chester commented as he entered the office in his white physician's coat. "Do you have back pain that needs treating?"

"No, Chester," she said, quickly straightening her spine like the model of the skeleton. "What did you want to show me?"

"Wait here," he said with a glint in his eye. He left for a few seconds and then reappeared with a well-dressed professional woman who immediately extended her hand to Rachel.

"Rachel, meet Darlene, my future wife," Chester said with pride.

Rachel warmly shook the hand of Chester's bride-to-be and then gave Chester a hug.

"You did good, Chester," she whispered in his ear.

"Rachel, your interviews were most enlightening," Chester said. "I saw the protective wall I had erected around myself over the years. And how emotionally closed I was. Had I continued in that vein, I would have died single." He took Darlene's hand in his. "Now I have a beautiful woman to share my heart."

Rachel left Chester's office feeling an inner joy about her work on the study. She realized that she hadn't ruined the study. Her sex interviews had benefited the lives of two men.

She climbed into her Valiant and put her key in the ignition, expecting the engine to sputter. But her car started up as though it were brand-new. When the tow-truck driver had told her that Johnny Wells had voluntarily repaired her car, for a second her heart had leaped. It was the kind of gesture that Zane would've made for her. She'd almost made herself believe that Zane was still alive.

But as she drove back to the university, a profound sadness filled her heart. The sex study had almost miraculously altered her life, too. She'd found the fondest love of her life. How could Zane really be gone? She still couldn't accept it.

Upon entering the university cafeteria, Rachel immediately searched for Kim. Kim was waiting at a table for her with blueberry muffins and coffee. The manila envelope was in her hand—the envelope she was anxiously waiting for. She knew it was crazy, but she prayed that the contents would reverse what she deep down knew to be true.

"I don't see the point of this, Rachel," Kim said. "Johnny Wells admitted to playing the role of Zane Farrell. What other proof do you need?"

"Something, anything," Rachel replied, hurting like a raw wound. "I still can't believe Zane's gone, Kim."

"If these papers can confirm whatever doubts you have, then I'm all for it," her friend said. "I hate seeing you suffer, Rachel."

Rachel anxiously unclasped the manila envelope. Her hands were trembling as she pulled out two sheets of paper and laid them side by side on the cafeteria table.

Each paper held the signature of Zane Farrell.

Her heartbeat raced, wanting both signatures to be the same. But her spirits dropped to her ankles. The signatures on the two sheets were entirely different.

On one paper, Zane Farrell's name was written in script as clear and neat as a schoolteacher's. On the other, his signature was scrawled illegibly, except for the *Z* for Zane and *F* for Farrell.

Rachel could feel her heart slow down its beat. It was true. Oh, God, it was true! The paper was the physical proof. Zane was never Zane at all.

"I had to beg Charlie to get me a copy of the real Zane Farrell's meticulously neat signature from the company file," Kim said. "And the careless signature was on the sex-study release form that Johnny Wells had to sign after your first interview."

"It's over, Kim," Rachel said tightly, tearing up both sheets of paper into tiny bits and hurling them into the trash can.

Kim wanted to talk more, but Rachel couldn't. She could barely remember thanking Kim for getting the signatures for her. Then she headed for her next class. She'd hoped the signatures would settle her emotions. Zane wasn't Zane. She finally had to accept the concrete truth of it.

But Rachel felt more distraught than ever.

How was she going to forget the sensual loving world she'd entered? How could she return to the self she was before her body and soul were lit up by—who?

If she hadn't fallen in love with Zane Farrell, who *had* she fallen so hard for?

Not the auto mechanic Johnny Wells.

The friendly voices of her students greeted her as she entered the lecture hall. No more Zane Farrell fantasies. No more dreams of tinkling wedding bells. Zane Farrell was dead.

"Johnny, you do not want more guacamole?" Tito's wife, Zoila, asked in a concerned voice at the dinner table in their lively colorful home. Tito's kids were laughing and talking amongst themselves. "Johnny, you hardly touched my food. You do not like?"

"I love your cooking, Zoila," Johnny quickly told her. "Your food is delicious. Please forgive me. My appetite's messed up, that's all."

Tito turned to his wife and said something in Spanish that Johnny wasn't supposed to understand. But Tito forgot about his brief Spanish lessons to Johnny for the Mexico trip.

Johnny knew that Tito was telling his wife that he had love problems. He saw Zoila shake her head in sympathy.

Johnny averted Zoila's empathetic gaze. He didn't want anyone feeling sorry for him. He was the one who'd screwed things up for himself. And now he had a gaping hole in his heart because of it.

"Johnny," Zoila began as she dished out another chicken taco onto his already-filled plate. "Have you talked to this woman you love since the trouble happened?"

"I tried calling her a few times," Johnny admitted as he fiddled with his fork. For the past few weeks, he'd left numerous messages on Rachel's university office answering machine.

"Johnny baby, why did you not tell me?" Tito asked.

"Because she hasn't returned any of my calls," Johnny said, swallowing hard. "Not one of them."

Tito's kids finished dinner and hurried from the table to do more fun things. The kitchen suddenly became quiet without their banter.

Johnny shifted uncomfortably in his seat. He'd always enjoyed sharing the warmth of Tito's family. Now it was like a torturous reminder that he was alone in life—very alone.

"She will talk to you," Zoila said in a reassuring tone. "If she loves you, she will not be able to resist."

"That's the problem, Zoila," Johnny said, putting down his fork. "She never loved *me*. She fell in love with *him*— Zane Farrell."

Zoila frowned, confused. "How can that be?" she said. "*You* were with her. *Your* heart was with her. *Your* body was with her. How can she love anybody but you?"

"Because I wasn't *being* me," Johnny replied, getting up from the table, frustrated at himself for being who he really was.

"You do not make sense, Johnny," Zoila said.

"Johnny boy, listen to my wife," Tito told him. "She is the brains of this family."

Johnny caught the eye-exchange of love between Tito and his wife, and the pain inside his heart cut even deeper. He'd had that love with Rachel. He'd been one with her, like Tito and Zoila were one.

"Johnny," Zoila said, interrupting his agonizing thoughts. "Maybe you wore rich clothes for her. Maybe you dined her expensive. Maybe you pretended to speak many, many knowledgeable things. But under that costume, you are Johnny Wells. And Johnny Wells is the man she loves. Why do you not see that?"

Johnny remained silent. He wanted so badly to believe her. But the burning guilt he felt about deceiving Rachel washed away any semblance of logic.

From the window, Johnny watched Tito's kids throwing a football back and forth to each other in the backyard. Tito's children who came from the deep love Tito shared with his wife. A love that grew from an honest place. An honest place Johnny had never experienced with Rachel.

"Mistakes can be undone, Johnny boy," Tito added. "You must forgive yourself. I know you well, Johnny. You're not the type of person to give up."

"Go ahead, call her again," Zoila advised. "A woman's heart is big. It can remain locked for only a short time. Then love flows out without any control of her own."

Johnny didn't know how to thank Tito and Zoila enough for their caring. He left Tito's house in his pickup truck feeling a trickle of hope. Maybe if he kept trying, Rachel would give him a chance to explain why he'd lied—and why he'd taken so long to get out the truth.

Once back at his Santa Monica apartment, Johnny hurriedly checked on his vegetable garden and then went straight to the phone. He dialed Rachel's home number, which he'd gotten from information, instead of using her office number where he'd left all of his past messages. He tensely waited for her to answer, hoping she'd give him that one chance.

"Hello?" Rachel's voice said into his ear.

His expectations rose. "Rachel, it's Johnny Wel—"

But her home answering machine voice droned on without hearing him. He couldn't let his excitement vanish. He had to keep up his pursuit of her. That's all he had left.

The machine beeped for his message.

"Rachel, please don't bypass my message," he quickly said. "Yes. I'm guilty of deceiving you. But I didn't do it deliberately. And I never meant to lead you on. Everything I ever said to you, everything I ever felt about you, is true. My feelings haven't changed about you, Rachel. Why won't you let me explain? I can't do it over an answering machine."

Johnny hung up, praying that maybe this once she'd return his call. One thing he knew for sure. If she didn't return this one, she'd hear from him tomorrow and the day after that and next week, too. He wasn't letting up until she heard what he had to say.

As Rachel entered her office, she struggled to put Johnny Wells's voice out of her mind. She couldn't believe that he'd dared to call her at home. He'd left a message of caring that she didn't dare allow herself to believe. She wasn't going to let him fool or humiliate her ever again.

In her hands she held the binder containing the entire sexuality research work, ready to be submitted to the administration. The study she'd put her heart and spirit into. The study that had fatally shattered a huge slice of her life.

"Rachel, come on, be proud of your hard work," Kim told her.

"I am," she replied and then added, "Sort of." The truth was, the research information didn't feel complete without her Zane Farrell interviews.

"Are you worried about what the chancellor will think?" Kim asked. "I already told him that Zane Farrell was not included in the research because he was out of the country at the time of your interviews, which is true. Chancellor Zilford understood completely. He's looking forward to reading your work."

"Thanks for covering for me, Kim," Rachel said, feeling grateful for such a dear friend.

"I wish I could do more for you, Rachel," Kim added. "Ever since Johnny Wells, the luster in your eyes has gone."

"I'll be okay, Kim. I just need a little more time."

Just then, Rachel's telephone rang. Rachel tensed up and didn't move to answer it. Kim was about to pick it up, but Rachel pulled her hand away.

"Please don't," Rachel pleaded. "Let the machine pick it up."

"Why?" Kim asked, confused.

When that familiar male voice resonated onto the answering machine, Rachel's body heat escalated. She fough he strong desire to pick up the phone and say, *Zane, oh, Zane, I've missed you so!*

"Rachel, I know you want me to stop bugging you," Johnny Wells began. "But I really need to talk to you. Why won't you hear me out? Please, Rachel."

Kim stared at her. "Pick it up, Rachel."

"I—I can't," she stammered. Her heart was hammering against her rib cage. She pulled the research papers tightly to her for emotional protection. "I just can't."

The machine clicked off.

"What are you afraid of, Rachel?" Kim asked. "It's over, isn't it? So what's the big deal about letting the man tell his side to clear his conscience?"

"I don't want to hear his explanations," she said in a shaky voice. "The entire matter is finished. It's in the past."

"Is it?" Her friend was staring at her as though she could see straight to her throbbing heart.

"Kim, I don't want to talk to Johnny Wells."

"But you miss him, Rachel."

"I miss the man I *thought* was Zane Farrell."

"Does the name really matter, Rachel?"

"Honesty and forthrightness does. And Johnny Wells doesn't possess either quality."

With that, Rachel carried the stack of research papers toward the door. "I'll meet you in the chancellor's office," was all she said.

But the moment Rachel was out of Kim's view, she bit her bottom lip so hard she could taste blood.

Why did Johnny Wells keep calling? Hearing his deep voice, the same manly resonating sound she'd associated with Zane Farrell, was sheer torture.

Because in her mind she didn't hear Johnny Wells. She heard Zane on the machine, the Zane she'd shared her heart with, the Zane she still ached to get naked and make love with again and again and again.

Rachel held the stack of research papers tightly to her chest, knowing all she had now was her profession. And as she headed toward the chancellor's office, she was determined to concentrate entirely on her career and not on her heart.

Johnny jumped out of his pickup at the university parking structure. He was set on facing Rachel flesh-to-flesh. After his last unanswered call to her office, he was through using the phone to reach her. He was going directly to the building where she worked.

Johnny hurried through the huge concourse with a determination he'd never possessed before. Rachel's not returning his calls had only infuriated him. At least she could have had the decency to call him back. Yet, even through his anger, he couldn't help smiling. Familiar with Rachel's stubborn will, he knew that she'd never give in without a battle. And a battle is what she'd get.

As Johnny stepped onto the lush green campus, his breath was wiped away. The magnificent university buildings stood in front of him with pride and dignity. Behind those walls were students soaking up ancient and modern knowledge that would change their lives and maybe even the future of the planet.

This was Rachel's academic world—a land in which Johnny felt like a foreigner.

Johnny reached the building that housed the offices of the sociology and psychology departments. Students and professors were rushing in and out.

As Johnny nervously entered the crowded hallway, he suddenly stopped walking. Down the hall was Rachel coming out of an office. She couldn't see him through the crowd of students whisking by.

Just seeing her sent a wave of hot emotion rushing into Johnny's chest. He wanted to grab her into his arms. He wanted to press her warm soft body against his. He wanted to tell her that he loved her.

But just then, a distinguished elderly gentleman in a charcoal suit and tie appeared right behind her. The gentleman vigorously shook Rachel's hand. A radiant smile came to her lips. Joining them was Kim, the scholarly-looking woman he'd seen picking up Rachel at the mansion for the birthday party. Kim happily hugged Rachel in a congratulatory manner.

Rachel was beaming as the distinguished gentleman and Kim spoke together in the hallway as students respectfully waved and greeted them.

The scholarly camaraderie between Rachel and her associates made Johnny feel on the outside. Rachel and her colleagues were college-degree holders who possessed trained intellects that Johnny could never match.

He leaned against the hallway wall watching them, students and professors rushing past him. How was he going to approach Rachel and her peers? What would he say to them? Yeah, sure, he could discuss the intricacies of brake pads, exhaust systems and fuel-injection philosophy. But he couldn't talk literature, social theory or higher mathematics.

Suddenly, Johnny felt someone nudge against him in the crowded hallway. He turned around to find a professorial man wearing spectacles and a suit and bow tie carrying thick textbooks under his arm.

"Excuse me, sir," the well-dressed man said to Johnny. He glanced at Johnny's dirty coveralls, lifted his spectacles higher on the bridge of his nose, and went on his way.

In the university atmosphere, Johnny knew that he stood out like a discarded piece of scrap metal amidst a treasure chest of shimmering gold.

Johnny saw Rachel wave goodbye to her associates and head in his direction through the crowd. A hurricane of emotional turmoil filled his body. His heart yearned to go to her, but his mind knew he was duping himself. Rachel could never accept him into her world. Johnny knew that truth now with his entire soul.

So before Rachel reached him, Johnny turned away with great despair in his heart. He headed out of the university building back to the repair shop where he belonged.

Rachel practically hopped like a bunny into her apartment. She closed and locked her door, threw her briefcase onto the sofa, and hurled her mail onto her small kitchen table.

"Yes!" she said with excitement.

She couldn't believe it! The chancellor shook *her* hand as though she was already a tenured professor. And he'd doubly complimented her outstanding work on the university sexuality study, even without Zane Farrell's case study.

Rachel practically skipped over to her answering machine and then halted. Though she told herself a zillion times that she wanted Johnny Wells to stop calling, her heartbeat quickened at the thought of hearing his voice again—the voice she still heard as Zane's.

She clicked on the machine to listen to her messages. She anxiously waited to hear the familiar manly voice that had sent tingles up and down her naked body while they made love in Mexico.

But the machine ended all its messages. Johnny Wells had not called.

She played back her messages. Maybe she hadn't listened carefully enough. But there was no sound of his voice.

Rachel sat down on a kitchen chair and stared blankly at the unopened bills and junk mail sitting on the table. All of the bubbly joy in her heart from the chancellor's congratulations was suddenly gone.

Johnny Wells had given up on her. She'd ignored his calls to the point where he'd had no other choice. Johnny Wells was out of her life for good.

Why didn't she feel relieved? She no longer had to feel angry about all his lies and deceit. She didn't have to suffer through any more reminders of her shameful uninhibited lovemaking to him.

Instead, Rachel felt a deep sadness flood her heart. And she suddenly felt very, very alone, knowing she'd never hear from him again.

Just then, her doorbell rang. A messenger handed her a beige envelope with her name gold-embossed on top. The courier was in a hurry, so she didn't have time to ask who it was from. She signed the release form and closed the door.

Rachel ran a finger over the gold embossing, feeling a tingle of excitement. For a second, she fantasized and pretended it was from Zane—the man she loved.

She hurriedly opened the envelope and pulled out a beige card made of fine-quality paper used for wedding invitations. When she opened the card, she saw Zane's signature scrawled at the bottom.

Her heart raced. But she quickly scolded herself for setting herself up for disappointment. This wasn't *her* Zane Farrell. The neat signature matched the one belonging to the real Zane Farrell she'd never met.

She slowly read the card.

Dear Professor Smith,
I am most sorry for the mistake made regarding my résumé being inadvertently E-mailed to the university for your research study. I am informed that my blunder caused you much inconvenience. Allow me to make it up to you. May I have your gracious presence for dinner at my home this Saturday evening with myself and my new bride. I do hope you will accept my invitation.

Most sincerely,
Zane Farrell.

Rachel read the card once again listening to the dignified tone of the note. Zane Farrell's diction was so poised and proper compared to Johnny Wells's version of him.

She realized that she liked Johnny Wells's informality better. His style was so down-to-earth, so raw, so masculine.

With Johnny's version, she'd rolled around naked and free, with sweat forming on her sexually hungry body, with her hair mussed and her clothes in disarray. She didn't have to worry about what he'd think. In fact, he'd savored that lustful part of her.

But Johnny Wells had left her life for good.

She held the gold-embossed card tightly between her fingertips. She'd have to say yes to Zane Farrell's invitation. It would be the proper thing to do.

But deep down, her heart and spirit ached for the pseudo–Zane Farrell. Why hadn't she returned any of Johnny Wells's calls? What was she afraid of?

She had to give Johnny Wells a chance to explain himself to her. She had to hear his truth.

She picked up the phone and dialed Zane's home phone number. But when she heard a strange voice answer, she quickly hung up, realizing she'd phoned the real Zane Farrell. Then she nervously dialed the repair-shop number that Johnny Wells had left on her message machine so many times. But a busy signal kept pounding at her ear, and she hung up.

Rachel knew what she had to do. After her dinner at Zane Farrell's house, she'd stop by Johnny Wells's shop and face his truth—if he still wanted her to listen.

Johnny slammed down the greasy shop phone. He tried to call Rachel again, but her home phone was busy. He couldn't stop himself. He needed to hear her voice, even though he'd vowed to forget her, even though he knew contacting her would end in futility.

Just then, a black stretch limousine pulled up to Johnny's auto repair shop. Mr. Farrell's chauffeur got out.

Johnny hadn't spoken to Mr. Farrell since his last phone conversation upon Mr. Farrell's arrival in L.A. with his bride-to-be.

"Johnny, Mr. Farrell would like a word with you," George told him.

"Sure," Johnny said. "Is he home? I'll call him right—"

George graciously cut in. "Mr. Farrell and his wife are waiting for you inside the car."

"Mr. Farrell wants to talk eye-to-eye with me?" Johnny asked, astounded. He'd always wanted to meet the man who'd saved his life. But he'd never dreamed he would.

George reached for the silver handle of the limo and opened the sleek charcoal door for Johnny. Johnny could see plush black carpeting, a bar, telephone, television set and computer screen. The passengers were well-hidden deep in the rear of the limo.

Johnny felt his palms perspiring. He didn't know what he'd say to the man who'd given him the heartfelt support he'd needed as a teenager. He'd gotten used to talking to Mr. Farrell over the phone, but to actually be in his honored presence . . . ?

"Johnny Wells, why do you keep us waiting?" Mr. Farrell's voice echoed from inside the stretch limo.

"No reason, Mr. Farrell," Johnny called out, and then he climbed aboard as George closed the door behind him.

Entering the limo palace, Johnny tried not to get the grime of his work clothes on the refined upholstery. When his eyes caught Mr. Farrell's, a simmering warmth filled his bones.

The elderly gentleman in front of Johnny was small in stature with sparse gray hair and a wrinkled face.

"Johnny Wells, how very good to see you," Mr. Farrell said with sparklingly alive slate-gray eyes.

"Mr. Farrell—" His voice caught, and his heart expanded inside his chest. How could he thank this man who'd been the only family he'd had?

"Johnny, meet my beautiful wife," Mr. Farrell said with pride. "She is the cause of my abandoning my vow of seclusion."

"Hello, Mrs. Farrell," Johnny said, gently shaking the hand of the graceful elderly woman beside him. Johnny's heart was singing. Mr. Farrell deserved all the happiness there was in life—and even more. "Mrs. Farrell, you are married to an incredible man."

"Oh, yes, I am well aware of that," she said.

Mr. Farrell tenderly took his bride's hand and lovingly squeezed it. His gray eyes twinkled as he looked at his wife, reminding Johnny of how he used to look at Rachel and of the intense love they'd shared.

Johnny glanced out the tinted car window at his repair shop. His work had to be his only love now. And he damn well better get used to it.

"Johnny, my wife and I are moving permanently to Paris as of today," Mr. Farrell went on. "Since you so successfully solved my accounting and real-estate problems, I must repay the favor."

"Repay me?" Johnny repeated incredulously. "Mr. Farrell, you've done too much for me already. What can I do for you?"

"You are an honorable man, Johnny Wells," Mr. Farrell continued. "I am proud to think of you as my son."

"Mr. Farrell, I owe you my life," Johnny told him. "I've been saving money for you. It's only a small part of what I owe you. But before you leave, I want to give it to you."

Mr. Farrell smiled. Johnny thought he saw a cloud of tears in his aging eyes.

"My boy," Mr. Farrell said, "you have given me such joy I cannot say. Keep those savings for yourself. I have ordered my accountant to transfer the property deed of my Bel

Air estate and the ownership documents of my red Porsche to your name.''

"You can't do that, Mr. Farrell," Johnny protested. "I won't accept it."

"Johnny Wells, you are too proud a man," Mr. Farrell said with knowledgeable eyes. "I shall regard a refusal on your part as a personal insult."

Just then, George opened the door to the limo. Johnny realized that Mr. Farrell had deemed their meeting over.

But Johnny didn't move.

"Please let me do something for you, Mr. Farrell," Johnny asked. "Something to let you know how much it's meant to me having you—like a father."

Then Johnny reached over and hugged the elderly man whose heart was bigger than the universe.

"Johnny Wells, be well," Mr. Farrell said. "You are a good man." But before the limousine door closed, Mr. Farrell added, "Make sure to be at your new house this Saturday evening. I have a surprise for you."

As the glossy black limousine drove away from Johnny's shop for the last time, he felt his chest tighten with sadness. He'd never before met a man as generous as Mr. Farrell, and he knew he never would again. He closed his fingers over the home and car keys that George had slipped into his hand before they left—the keys to his new life.

But a bittersweet taste came into Johnny's mouth. Now he had the mansion and Porsche. He had a well-nourished bank account. His life had taken on mini–Zane Farrell proportions. But Johnny was still Johnny. And he didn't have the one thing that would truly make his life rich. He didn't have Professor Rachel Smith.

The headlights on Rachel's Valiant lit up the Bel Air road in front of her. She turned up the rock music on her radio to try to block out the trepidation rising within her like a tornado. As she approached the open King Kong gates of

Zane Farrell's property, she slowed her foot on the gas pedal.

She knew she should turn her car around, return to her apartment, and call Mr. Farrell to say she had to work late or wasn't feeling very well. She dreaded stepping foot into his emotionally charged house. The place where she fell in love with Johnny Wells.

Rachel drove through the gates and parked her car in front of the mansion. She turned off the engine and sat for a long moment trying to gain control of her heartbeat and breathing.

Maybe seeing the face of the real Zane Farrell would knock her back to ice-cold reality. Yes, she desperately needed to meet this man. His presence would make it Plexiglas clear to her that the love in her heart was a farce.

With trembling fingers, Rachel rang the bell of the familiar double copper doors.

The door flew open Zane Farrell–style. Rachel's heart pounded uncontrollably in anticipation. But her eyes widened in fiery fury when she saw Johnny Wells standing there in greasy coveralls with oil-stained hands.

"What are *you* doing here?" Rachel demanded.

Her voice was shaky—not only because she was angrier than a raging lion, but just seeing Johnny Wells again brought back all the love and excitement she'd felt the first time she'd met him.

"I should ask what *you* are doing here," he replied with a twinkling glint to his famous sea-blues. He leaned both hands against the sides of the door frame, so near to her, so close to caressing her.

"Don't start that again," she snapped. "Where's Zane Farrell?"

"Mr. Farrell doesn't live here anymore," he replied. "He moved to Paris with his new wife."

"You tricked me into coming here, didn't you?" she went on, realizing that he hadn't changed. He'd never change.

"That engraved invitation I got was a hoax. Just like all the other distortions and untruths you've thrown at me!"

"Invitation?" he repeated, confused. "What invitation?"

"Stop playing games with me," she insisted. "I'm not the naive professor anymore. I know your manipulative ways."

"I didn't send you any invitation," he said, his voice rising. Then his eyes lit up. "It was Mr. Farrell! He set it all up. He gave me his house and told me to be here knowing you would—"

"You're incapable of telling the truth," she accused him. "I don't need this!"

She turned around to charge out of there, but Johnny Wells grabbed her arm and whirled her to face him. His strong hands on her shoulders sent electrical currents through her veins. She could feel his minty breath on her face. She struggled to fight the urge to surrender completely to him.

"You know what's wrong with you, Professor Smith?" Johnny Wells began. "You don't want to hear the truth."

"That's ridiculous," she said defensively, wishing he wasn't touching her, wishing she didn't feel her legs buckling or her heart burning like a red-hot iron in her chest.

"Oh, yeah? Then why don't you believe that I didn't send you any invite? It was Mr. Farrell's way of getting us back together."

Johnny's fingers tightened on Rachel's shoulders. He wasn't letting her go now. "And you're going to listen to me this time. I had a commitment with Mr. Farrell to pretend to be him while I house-sat. I was obligated to keep to my word to him, even after I realized I was falling in love with you."

"Was *sex* part of your agreement, too?" she countered with challenging eyes.

"Is that what you think?" Johnny asked, stunned.

"You saw the opportunity and you grabbed it."

"You certainly didn't discourage me, did you?" he said, remembering her scalding kisses and inflamed lovemaking.

"Get away from me, Johnny Wells!" she cried, struggling to pull free of his grasp.

But Johnny pulled her closer. He saw the hurt in her soft oval eyes and hated himself for his cracks, knowing it was her most vulnerable spot.

"Are you blind, Rachel?" he said. "I love you. From the moment I opened Mr. Farrell's door, I loved you."

But Rachel only stared at him, not saying anything, and Johnny knew why. Dammit, he knew exactly why!

"I'm not asking that you love me back," Johnny managed to say. "I know I'm not the well-educated, well-read Mr. Farrell you fell for. And I'll never be the cultured, intellectual man you need."

Rachel shushed him with her fingertips. "It's not Zane Farrell I love," she whispered. "It's you—Johnny Wells. It's you I've always loved."

Johnny couldn't believe his ears. "But I'm just a car mechanic. Having this expensive house and a cool sports car won't change who I am, Rachel."

"Will you shut up and kiss me?" she said with misty eyes.

Johnny's heart was flying as he closed his mouth over hers. He felt her tongue dance and play with his. And he knew the love between them was real and solid and came from a concrete place not based on what he was but on who he was.

Rachel hungrily clasped her hands tightly around Johnny Wells's neck and pressed her eager body to his hard muscles. She felt as if she was home again. Her love for Johnny swelled her heart to gigantic proportions. She slid her hands down his rippling back and settled them on his buttocks. She pressed his growing bulge against her until a moan escaped from her lips.

Suddenly, one monumental thought savagely coursed through her consciousness. One torturous thought that she knew would plague her forever if she didn't ask.

"Johnny," Rachel whispered in his ear as she stood on tiptoes against his solid frame. "Are you sure you want to be with a sex maniac like me?"

Johnny leaned his head back to look deep into her eyes. His sea-blues were smiling down at her. "I'll prove it to you," he whispered back.

Then Johnny swooped her into his strapping arms and carried her up the lavender-carpeted staircase.

Rachel rested her lips against his broad neck as her body bounced with his every step. She could smell the sweat of the repair shop on his skin, and the workman scent made her desire him even more.

He carried her into the master bedroom and gently laid her on the satiny circular bed.

"I've been fantasizing about this ever since the house tour," Johnny said huskily.

He expertly slipped off her dress, unclasped her lacy bra and pulled down her French-cut panties. Then he openly gazed at her vulnerable nakedness pulsating against the velvety white satin sheets.

"You're beautiful," he groaned. "So so beautiful."

As his eyes caressed her breasts and feminine spot, the sensitive area between Rachel's thighs throbbed with yearning for him.

Her breathing quickened as she watched Johnny strip off his work shirt and coveralls. His naked broad chest and huge manhood were before her eyes.

"Johnny, I want you," she whispered in a deep voice, liking the sound of his name, loving that he was with her now.

Johnny knelt beside the circular bed and spread her legs apart. She gasped as he slid both thumbs up the length of her inner thighs.

When his fingers reached the feminine patch between her legs, she arched up to meet him. As he caressed her pleasure spot, he slipped inside her feminine opening. Electrical explosions radiated throughout her every limb.

"Johnny!" she groaned. "Oh, Johnny!"

Johnny explored and massaged until her groaning became louder and louder, and she clutched his hair, twisting the curls between her fingers in erotic ecstasy.

Johnny glanced up at her as his fingers hungrily enjoyed her. Her eyes intertwined with his in a spiritual oneness. And she knew he loved satisfying her.

Suddenly, Johnny lifted her off the bed into his strong arms.

"Here's another fantasy of mine," he said hoarsely as his mouth grazed against her lips.

Johnny carried her into the master bathroom and set her down on the tiled floor. He opened the clear-glassed shower door and turned on the water of both faucets until the temperature was cozy warm.

"Now you can't say you've never taken a shower with a man," he whispered in a gravelly voice. His naked member stood huge and stiff in front of her.

As she stepped under the trickling water, Johnny joined her wet body and closed the shower door behind them.

With an earnestness, he soaped up both massive hands and covered her throbbing breasts with foam. He massaged, squeezed and kneaded her swollen nipples with his soapy fingertips.

Rachel held her breath at his hot touch, and unable to hold herself back a moment longer, she bubbled up her hands with soap and reached for his hard manliness.

"I forgot to ask you a question for the study," she began, her breathing increasing in short gasps. "Do you like to be massaged by a woman?"

Johnny's yes answer was a low groan from the depth of his throat as she slid her soapy hands up and down his expanded masculinity. She pressed his private area against her stomach and then between her aching breasts.

And then her lips intimately touched his body.

"Rachel—" Johnny gasped as she performed rapid movements on him until he thought he was going to explode. He leaned his head back into the shower spray to try to restrain the release yearning to take place.

"I need to be inside you," he groaned.

He gripped her naked wet waist and spun her body around so her firm buttocks faced him. As he bent her over a little, he gently merged with her.

"Ohhhh!" Rachel cried out in uninhibited pleasure.

The shower sprayed onto the steamy glass as Johnny delved deeper inside her, holding her hips with his bare hands.

His manliness filled her completely as he moved in and out. He reached around in front of her and caressed her pleasure zone until he felt her contract over and over.

Suddenly, he couldn't hold back any longer. As he groaned out loud, his juices spewed forth into the depths of her body.

As the water sprinkled down on them, Johnny gently kissed Rachel's mouth, cheeks, eyes and chin. He couldn't get enough of her sweetness.

"I love you, Rachel," Johnny whispered, knowing the words fell so very short of expressing how deeply he felt for her.

"Johnny, I love you, too," she whispered back as she pressed her wet body against his. "I'm so happy, Johnny, so happy!"

The sound of Rachel's joyful words vibrated in his head like a message from heaven. Rachel loved him! Him— Johnny Wells. He squeezed her tightly against him as he turned off the water. Then he reached for a cotton towel and began to dry off her face, her dripping hair, and then covered her full breasts with slow caressing strokes.

Rachel bathed in his erotic towel motion. As he slid the towel farther down between her legs and dried her ecstasy area with deliberate strokes, she murmured, "Mmm, maybe we ought to take another shower."

She was ready for more of Johnny Wells, much, much more. Her body was suddenly hotter with arousal than before they'd made love. Having sex with him had only made her desire him more.

Suddenly, a familiar ring of warning entered her head, a warning that she couldn't make go away.

"Johnny, what if—what if I want to make love to you ten more times today?"

"Rachel, Rachel," Johnny began, dropping the towel and letting his bare finger enter the yearning opening between her thighs. "I can sexually take you on twenty, thirty times every day of your life. Are we on?"

"Yes, yes, yes!" she happily replied, running her hands over his tight-muscled abdomen and slowly slipping her palms downward to his masculine part.

"On one condition," Johnny added with a mischievous glint in his sea-blues.

"Oh, I hate your conditions!"

"Are you allergic to car oil?" he asked.

"No," she replied, getting aroused at the erotic possibilities he might have in mind.

"How about battery fluid?"

"Sounds tempting to me," she replied with a giggle.

"No objections to sex lunches behind the closed door of my shop office?"

"I look forward to it."

"Good," Johnny said, pulling her pelvis against his rock-hard muscle. "Will you become my wife?"

"What took you so long to ask?" she replied.

Rachel flipped on the shower spray. "Ready for more?"

Johnny grinned as he went under the sprinkling water, taking her throbbing body with him.

As Rachel gobbled up Johnny's delicious body, she closed her eyes and forgot her inhibitions, reservations and restraints.

All she was aware of was the ecstatic pleasure of sexual union with the man she loved—Johnny Wells.

*   *   *   *   *

This October, be the first to read these wonderful authors as they make their dazzling debuts!

**THE WEDDING KISS by Robin Wells
(Silhouette Romance #1185)**
A reluctant bachelor rescues the woman he loves from the man she's about to marry—and turns into a willing groom himself!

**THE SEX TEST by Patty Salier
(Silhouette Desire #1032)**
A pretty professor learns there's more to making love than meets the eye when she takes lessons from a sexy stranger.

**IN A FAMILY WAY by Julia Mozingo
(Special Edition #1062)**
A woman without a past finds shelter in the arms of a handsome rancher. Can she trust him to protect her unborn child?

**UNDER COVER OF THE NIGHT by Roberta Tobeck
(Intimate Moments #744)**
A rugged government agent encounters the woman he has always loved. But past secrets could threaten their future.

**DATELESS IN DALLAS by Samantha Carter
(Yours Truly)**
A hapless reporter investigates how to find the perfect mate—and winds up falling for her handsome rival!

Don't miss the brightest stars of tomorrow!

Only from ▼ *Silhouette*®

WTW

Take 4 bestselling love stories FREE

Plus get a FREE surprise gift!

As seen on TV!
Free Gift Offer

With a Free Gift proof-of-purchase from any Silhouette® book,
you can receive a beautiful cubic zirconia pendant.

This gorgeous marquise-shaped stone is a genuine cubic
zirconia—accented by an 18" gold tone necklace.

(Approximate retail value $19.95)

Send for yours today...
compliments of ▼ *Silhouette*®

To receive your free gift, a cubic zirconia pendant, send us one original proof-of-purchase, photocopies not accepted, from the back of any Silhouette Romance™, Silhouette Desire®, Silhouette Special Edition®, Silhouette Intimate Moments® or Silhouette Yours Truly™ title available in August, September or October at your favorite retail outlet, together with the Free Gift Certificate, plus a check or money order for $1.65 U.S./$2.15 CAN. (do not send cash) to cover postage and handling, payable to Silhouette Free Gift Offer. We will send you the specified gift. Allow 6 to 8 weeks for delivery. Offer good until October 31, 1996 or while quantities last. Offer valid in the U.S. and Canada only.

Free Gift Certificate

Name: _____

Address: _____

City: _____ State/Province: _____ Zip/Postal Code: _____

Mail this certificate, one proof-of-purchase and a check or money order for postage and handling to: SILHOUETTE FREE GIFT OFFER 1996. In the U.S.: 3010 Walden Avenue, P.O. Box 9077, Buffalo NY 14269-9077. In Canada: P.O. Box 613, Fort Erie, Ontario L2Z 5X3.

FREE GIFT OFFER   084-KMD

ONE PROOF-OF-PURCHASE

To collect your fabulous FREE GIFT, a cubic zirconia pendant, you must include this original proof-of-purchase for each gift with the properly completed Free Gift Certificate.

084-KMD

Your very favorite Silhouette miniseries characters now have a BRAND-NEW story in

CHRISTMAS KISSES

Brought to you by:

LINDA HOWARD

DEBBIE MACOMBER

LINDA TURNER

LINDA HOWARD celebrates the holidays with a **Mackenzie** wedding—once Maris regains her memory, that is....

DEBBIE MACOMBER brings **Those Manning Men** and **The Manning Sisters** home for a mistletoe marriage as a single dad finally says "I do."

LINDA TURNER brings **The Wild West** alive as Priscilla Rawlings ties the knot at the Double R Ranch.

Three BRAND-NEW holiday love stories...by romance fiction's most beloved authors.

Available in November at your favorite retail outlet.

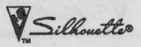